WHOSE WEDDING?

Sara stepped forward from the counter. "Stop shouting," she begged. "Both of you. Please...!"

"And I suppose I should have let you run off into the night like a pair of ... gypsies!" Hetty spat out the word as if it tasted like poison. "I wanted you to have the kind of wedding you could be proud of!

"No! Oh no! You did not!" Olivia retorted, spinning around to look at Hetty with angry tears in her eyes. "You wanted a wedding that *you* would be proud of, Hetty King! Well, whose wedding is this anyway, mine or yours?"

Sara swallowed hard. There was no going back now. Her Aunt Olivia had mouthed what Sara knew had been in her heart all week long, and a huge silence reigned.

Also available in the Road to Avonlea Series from Bantam Skylark books

The Ties That Bind

Storybook written by

Heather Conkie

Based on the Sullivan Films Production
written by Heather Conkie
adapted from the novels of

Lucy Maud Montgomery

A BANTAM SKYLARK BOOK®
NEW YORK · TORONTO · LONDON · SYDNEY · AUCKLAND

Based on the Sullivan Films Production produced by Sullivan Films Inc.
in association with CBC and the Disney Channel with the participation
of Telefilm Canada adapted from Lucy Maud Montgomery's novels.

Teleplay written by Heather Conkie
Copyright © 1991 by Sullivan Films Distribution, Inc.

This edition contains the complete text
of the original edition.
NOT ONE WORD HAS BEEN OMITTED.

RL 6, 008–012

THE TIES THAT BIND
A Bantam Skylark Book / published by arrangement with
HarperCollins Publishers Ltd.

PUBLISHING HISTORY
HarperCollins edition published 1994
Bantam edition / March 1994

ROAD TO AVONLEA is the trademark of Sullivan Films Inc.

Skylark Books is a registered trademark of Bantam Books,
a division of Bantam Doubleday Dell Publishing Group, Inc.
Registered in U.S. Patent and Trademark Office and elsewhere.

ISBN 0-553-48120-7

Bantam Books are published by Bantam Books, a division of Bantam Doubleday Dell
Publishing Group, Inc. Its trademark, consisting of the words "Bantam Books" and the
portrayal of a rooster, is Registered in U.S. Patent and Trademark Office and in other
countries. Marca Registrada. Bantam Books, 1540 Broadway, New York, New York 10036.

PRINTED IN THE UNITED STATES OF AMERICA
OPM 0 9 8 7 6 5 4 3 2 1

Chapter One

A week to the day before their June wedding, Olivia King and Jasper Dale pedaled their bicycle-built-for-two along the rolling and winding road that led from Avonlea to Golden Milestone, the Dale farm.

The sight had become quite a familiar one to the residents of the little Prince Edward Island village. Olivia and Jasper, together on the bicycle Jasper had invented especially for them, sometimes with photographic equipment hanging from their shoulders as they went off to record history for the Avonlea *Chronicle*, sometimes just as they were now, pedaling as one, enjoying their comfortable solitude in the peace and quiet of the countryside.

The people of Avonlea still thought Jasper was an odd duck, too much prone, in their opinion, to tinkering and inventing, but they recognized his differences now with tolerance and a certain respect. They often pointed out this two-seated bicycle contraption of his with genuine pride, saying a better one couldn't be had, even from the catalogues that arrived twice yearly in the Lawsons' general store. Jasper Dale was a strange fellow for sure, but he had a head full of knowledge and more curiosity than a jaybird, and you never knew what he would come up with next.

Jasper Dale's failures and successes were the topic of many heated discussions around the pot-bellied stove in the general store. No one could agree on which Jasper escapade was more entertaining— the day he and his "amazing" flying machine had ended up in the haystack in the King pasture, or the fateful evening his magic-lantern show had set fire to the Town Hall. But the one thing that everyone in town agreed on was that he was darn lucky to have met up with Olivia King. She was the best thing that had ever happened to him.

As Olivia pedaled along, with the fresh sea breeze in her face and the blur of orange devil's paintbrushes and purple lupine passing beside her against the deep-blue sky, the lady in question herself would have heartily disagreed. On the contrary, she believed the best thing that had ever happened to her was Jasper Dale.

She leaned forward and called to him above the crunch of the gravel beneath their wheels. "Oh Jasper, I hope the weather is as beautiful as this next Saturday!"

Jasper's knuckles tightened on the handlebars and the bike wavered in the soft ruts of the road. Was it really that close? Next Saturday? He let his breath out in a slow whistle and tried to ignore the fact that his chest was suddenly tight. But it was no use. Despite the fresh air pouring through his lungs, he felt sure he was suffocating.

Olivia couldn't help but notice the sudden stiffening of Jasper's back, but, looking over his shoulder, she attributed it to the sight that met their eyes as they reached the crest of the hill and looked down upon the Dale farm. It was an unaccustomed beehive of activity.

Felix King was mowing the lawn. His older sister Felicity and their cousin Sara Stanley were busy weeding the front garden. A man whose face Olivia didn't recognize was perched precariously on the roof of the house replacing shingles. Mr. Biggins and two boys from the village were setting up ladders to paint the barn, and two other fellows were already painting the fence and the rose arbor. Jasper and Olivia pedaled into the yard and looked around in amazement.

"What are all these people doing here?" asked Jasper quietly after dismounting the bicycle and leaning it against the only surface of the fence that wasn't being sanded down or painted.

"I don't know…I…" stammered Olivia, not quite sure how to break the news to her fiancé that these sorts of things were necessary before a wedding. "Oh yes," she said brightly, as if remembering for the first time. "I asked Mr. Owens to fix the roof…it had to be repaired before the…you know…wedding. Oh, and Felix said he'd do the lawn…for a price, of course. I knew you wouldn't have time to do it," she hastened to add, noticing that Jasper's face was becoming shiny with little drops of perspiration.

"Seems like a lot of fuss," was all he managed to say as he extracted a handkerchief from his pocket and wiped his brow. Jasper hated crowds. He was extremely shy by nature, and this invasion of his privacy was almost more than he could bear, even for Olivia's sake, and there was *nothing* he wouldn't do for her.

Unaware of how deeply distressed Jasper was, Olivia smiled at him fondly and gave his hand a little squeeze. "Even the simplest things take preparation."

Mr. Biggins was in the middle of giving lengthy instructions to one of the boys on the proper way to ready a fence post for painting when he looked up and caught sight of the happy couple. He left his obviously relieved helper and ambled over to them, his sunburned arm outstretched to shake the hand of the groom-to-be. Jasper took it damply.

"Now," Mr. Biggins boomed heartily, "do you want all four sides of the barn painted, or just the side that shows?" He laughed at his own attempt at humor and waited for a decision.

"Well, I don't know," said Olivia, her soft brown eyes looking up at Jasper from under her long lashes. "What do you think, Jasper?"

Jasper couldn't meet her gaze. He found it very disconcerting at the moment. He made some flapping gestures in the general direction of his barn. "Uh...well...just the...sides that...just the sides that..."

"Fine and dandy!" said Mr. Biggins, slapping poor Jasper on the back and turning to go back to work. "I've put my paint and rags and stuff in the barn, Jasper," he called back over his shoulder. "Hope you don't mind."

Jasper snapped to attention. "Oh...no...there's a lot of fragile equipment in there," he protested. "I wouldn't want it to get..."

Mr. Biggins waved his fears away. "The boys and I were real careful!" he called back cheerily as he continued on his way.

"Oh…I'm sure you were…" said Jasper to the man's receding back. "I'll just go and…check," he mumbled to Olivia, his face a cloud of misery. "Excuse me…" He said, leaving his confused fiancé watching him as he literally ran to the barn.

"Aunt Olivia! Felicity and I have all the flowers planned. We found a beautiful patch of Queen Anne's Lace behind Mrs. Biggins's boarding house, and she has promised not to let her husband mow it down!" Sara Stanley's face shone as she looked up at her aunt. When no reaction was forthcoming, she followed her gaze to the barn, where Jasper had disappeared.

"That's lovely, Sara," Olivia replied absently. *Obviously distracted by love itself*, thought her niece, her blond head full of the romantic notions that only a wedding can conjure up.

"Just think, Aunt Olivia, in one week, you'll be Mrs. Jasper Dale!"

Olivia swallowed hard, amazed as always at the rush of emotion that hit her like a wave every time she heard those words, "Mrs. Jasper Dale." She smiled down at Sara and gave her a big hug. "I know!" she breathed, totally happy and immensely sad, feeling the heady promise of the future and the bitter pang of departure at the very same moment.

"Sara!" Felicity's voice called from the garden. Sara gave her favorite aunt a hug and a squeeze and ran back to join her cousin.

Olivia looked around at the transformation that was taking place before her eyes. The Dale farm had become decidedly run-down over the years, and Jasper, caught up in his own interests, didn't mind one way or the other. Olivia didn't either, for that matter. She loved her future home, shabby or not. But somehow, having a wedding there, seeing it through the eyes of their guests and, of course, her family, put it in a different light.

Olivia was still lost in her own thoughts when the sound of buggy wheels jolted her back to reality.

Hetty King pulled into the yard and briskly pulled on the reins, bringing her horse to a stop. She looked around at the hustle and bustle from under her hat brim, placed *just so* on her impeccable coiffure. Without saying a word, her entire being implied that she was singularly unimpressed. She had perfected this look over the years. As the revered teacher of the Avonlea school, she found it came in very handy with both students and parents.

Olivia took a deep breath, smiled a welcome and walked over to her older sister.

"Hetty!" she greeted her brightly. "What good timing. I need some advice."

Hetty King arched one eyebrow and looked down at Olivia with a smirk.

"Advice? How unusual."

Hetty was still smarting from a conversation she had had with Olivia only a few days after her engagement to Jasper Dale had been announced. Her usually agreeable younger sister had made it quite clear to her that she wanted no interference with the plans for her wedding. She wanted to do it her way. Hetty sniffed disdainfully at the memory. So be it. Let her do it—*her* way.

Olivia smiled, refusing to be put off. "Where do you think we should set up the picnic after the ceremony?"

"Olivia," began Hetty grandly, "far be it from me to give you any advice about your wedding. I swore right from the start that I wouldn't interfere, and I haven't."

Olivia refused to rise to the bait. "I appreciate that…" she began, but Hetty had only just begun to warm up.

"Did I object when you announced that you wouldn't need a wedding gown?" she asked, a cold smile still fixed upon her face. "Did I rant and rave when you decided to be married in front of a barn, instead of in the church where every other

King for generations has been married, even if it will be the singular most embarrassing moment of my entire life? No, I did not."

Olivia took a deep breath. "Hetty…I know we feel differently about—"

"If you want to stand up in an everyday dress, clutching a bunch of weeds—"

"Wildflowers, Hetty," said Olivia tersely, still trying to maintain her composure.

"Weeds, Olivia," Hetty snapped. "Then that's your business. I simply stopped by to see if you want a ride home."

"No, thank you," replied Olivia, barely able to be civil. "I'm going to stay here for a while longer. There's still a lot to be done. We could use some help …"

"I daresay you could," replied Hetty, glancing around the property in her most haughty manner. She gave the reins a little flick and set off along the drive to the road, not once looking back, her posture erect and unmoving.

Olivia sighed and walked away towards the outbuildings.

The sun streamed through the high windows of the barn, sending shafts of light through the still, dusty air. In a dim corner at a workbench, Jasper sat with his head bent over a model airplane. The swinging wooden door creaked and he looked up to see Olivia enter, her expression a reflection of how he felt.

"Honestly, Jasper. Hetty can be so exasperating, so…so holier-than-thou…" Olivia paused, noticing his deep concentration. "What happened?" She walked over to him, stepping carefully to avoid knocking over any of his baskets of bits and pieces. To an untrained eye, they were hopeless piles of junk, but on close inspection, they were all carefully labeled and sorted,

Jasper looked at Olivia over the rims of his wire glasses. "Oh, I suppose one of the boys couldn't resist giving this a throw…" he said lightly, trying to make it sound as if it were nothing, but the desperately disappointed look in his eyes was unmistakable. The forlorn model airplane sat on the workbench in pieces.

Olivia reached his side and put a sympathetic hand on his shoulder.

"Oh Jasper, I'm so sorry…" she mumbled, knowing full well that if it hadn't been for her, there would be no strangers invading the farm, handling and breaking his belongings.

"Don't you be sorry," said Jasper, immediately distressed that he had upset her. "It's just…a lot of people milling around…"

"You don't like it, do you?" asked Olivia quietly.

Jasper turned and faced her. "Like what?"

"The idea of having the wedding here. All the people …"

Jasper started to speak but Olivia put her finger to his lips. "Jasper, listen to me. We don't have to go through with all this if you don't want to. All that matters to me is that we get married."

Jasper looked deep into Olivia's determined eyes and realized that she meant it.

Chapter Two

The sun sank behind the fields of hay on the King farm, its light making the swaying stalks into spun gold for that moment before they were lost in the purple and blue shadows of dusk. On the hill among the apple trees, lamps were lit in the white clapboard house, and the sound of dinner dishes clattering in the sink mixed with the cooing and gurgling of a baby.

The King household was a picture of family bliss. Janet King was trying her best to feed applesauce to a squirming baby Daniel, and Alec was washing up the dinner plates. Janet wiped her youngest son's face for the umpteenth time and chuckled along with his obvious delight in discovering the gooey consistency of his dessert.

Alec looked up from the soapy water and

enjoyed the relative silence of the house.

"I suppose things will be turned upside down around here over the next few days," he said dolefully.

"Oh now Alec, don't worry," said Janet, successfully shoveling more fruit into Daniel's mouth and spilling very little. "Everything's under control. I've figured it all out, and there's plenty of room."

"I'm almost glad Andrew and Roger can't make it," mumbled Alec. His brother Roger had recently taken a job at Dalhousie University in Halifax, and his nephew Andrew had joined him there. Presently, they were both on an archaeological dig somewhere in South America, an opportunity that Roger had found difficult to turn down and Olivia had insisted he take. South America was exactly where he'd like to be himself over the next week or so, Alec thought ruefully.

"Alec King!" scolded Janet softly, almost as if she had read his thoughts, but a smile played on her lips as she watched her husband putting the cups and saucers away.

"I only mean..." Alec struggled with his former train of thought. "Goodness knows where we would have put them..."

"And I certainly didn't hear Hetty volunteering to take them," added Janet wryly.

"Ah well, that's one thing we don't need to worry about anyway," said Alec. "I suppose you've heard from your Aunt Eliza?" he added with some hesitation.

"You know I did," replied Janet. "She wrote a lovely long letter. Great-Aunt Eliza wouldn't miss a wedding for the world."

"Hmmm ..." was all Alec said.

"She's an old dear and you know it," chided Janet.

Alec came up behind her and gave her a hug. "Those aren't exactly the words that jump to my mind, but I promise to behave myself. I don't know how you manage to do it all. You're a wonder."

Baby Daniel beamed with pleasure and gurgled, applesauce spilling charmingly from the sides of his mouth. He attempted to get it back in the right place with his fingers and instead found that they were equally as delicious as the applesauce. The two parents were entranced. To Daniel's delight, they laughed and coochie-cooed at him. So engrossed were they with the baby that they failed to notice ten-year-old Cecily, their youngest daughter, tiptoeing into the pantry and scooping up the scraps that Alec had just scraped from the dinner plates.

"I'm so glad that Olivia decided to keep the wedding simple," Janet said, giving Daniel's face a final wipe.

Alec smiled and shook his head. "I don't think it's simple enough for Jasper's taste. I saw him in town today. He looked like a man about to go to the gallows."

While her parents were still involved in their conversation, Cecily grabbed the opportunity to sneak out the back door with the heaping plate of scraps. She closed the screen door as quietly as possible, taking care that it didn't slam against the frame as it usually did when any of the King children left the house.

It was dark outside but for the glow of light from the kitchen, and there wasn't a sound except for the frogs in the nearby pond and the crickets in her mother's vegetable garden.

Cecily crouched down with the plate of goodies. "Here puppy. C'mon boy," she called softly.

Within seconds, there was a faint rustling in the bushes and a huge, shaggy, matted, golden-haired dog appeared from out of the shadows. It paced and circled for a wary moment and then came forward, wagging its tail at Cecily expectantly. Spying the plate, it instantly went to work, gobbling down the leftovers.

Cecily patted its filthy fur. "Good dog. Are you lost?" she crooned, and the dog licked her face in appreciation. Cecily wrinkled her nose. In spite of her adoring love for any stray, even she knew this dog could use a bath.

The crickets and frogs chorused outside the Dale farm as well, but the only stray creature that paced and circled there was Jasper. In his study, clocks of all shapes and sizes, hanging on the walls, perched on shelves and sitting on tables, ticked steadily and rhythmically, all but drowning out nature's competition.

Jasper was normally very proud of his collection of clocks, but at this moment they were making him extremely edgy. For the tenth time in as many minutes, he nervously fished his father's old watch from his vest pocket and, after intently examining the mantel clock, the most dependable in his experience, he minutely adjusted the hands on its face, synchronizing them exactly. He snapped the gold cover shut, put it neatly back where it had come from, cleaned his glasses fastidiously, pulled on his jacket and left the room with the air of a man setting out on an extremely secret and danger-ous mission.

Chapter Three

Hetty King closed the book she was reading with a snap. She suddenly realized how late it must be. Sara had gone to bed more than an hour ago, and Olivia had been as quiet as a mouse at dinner and had retired early, complaining of a headache. What did she know of headaches? thought Hetty, somewhat unkindly. She stood and stretched her back and neck, noticing how tense she had become lately. It was no wonder, with all this wedding nonsense going on. She blew out the lamp on the table with gusto and prepared to go to bed. She was halfway up the stairs before she decided that a cup of tea might be just the thing to take away her aches and pains.

Olivia King moved quietly to and fro in her tiny room under the eaves at Rose Cottage. She heard a step on the stairs and stood stock-still, holding her breath. Only when she heard the footsteps retreat towards the kitchen did she relax. She looked around her bedroom. The faded wallpaper with its tiny sprays of violets and lilacs, the white lace curtains, the small painting over her bed of the titian-haired child swimming in a moonlit pond—all were as familiar to her as her own face. She had slept and dreamed in this room since she was a child.

Olivia shook herself from her reverie and continued with the job at hand. She folded a blue taffeta dress carefully and put it in the small valise that lay open on her bed. From her top drawer, hidden under a pile of sensible underthings, she took out a beautiful white nightgown trimmed with handmade lace and blue ribbons. She gazed at it almost in disbelief for a moment and then hurriedly packed it. Over her shoulder she could feel Hetty's eyes on her. She whirled around. A photograph of her sister sat staring at her from the bureau. She hesitated and then turned it decisively face downward.

Outside in the darkness, a ladder was clumsily placed against the wall of Rose Cottage. The ground was soft and uneven, however, and a shadowy figure struggled desperately to steady it, almost losing his balance in the process. After much grunting and rustling of bushes, the ladder was finally placed as securely as it could be, its top rung reaching to a dark window on the second story.

The moon appeared from behind a scudding cloud and its light revealed the white, anxious face of Jasper Dale as he took a deep breath and started to climb. His knees were knocking so uncontrollably that it made for very slow progress.

Startled from sleep, Sara sat bolt upright in her bed. What was that noise? She threw back her eiderdown and tiptoed out into the hall.

As Hetty King carried her tea from the kitchen, she too heard a faint clatter from outside, and her ears pricked up.

Olivia's heart leapt at the first rustling in the bushes below, and she quietly lifted her window sash and leaned out. She fully expected to see the ladder directly below, but there was nothing. Slowly she turned. There indeed was her method of escape—up against the wrong window. Hetty's window, no less! Olivia sighed to herself and caught sight of Jasper clinging to the sides of the ladder, grim-faced in the shadows. She motioned wildly to him.

"Jasper, over here!" she whispered, as loudly as she dared.

Jasper swore softly, realizing his mistake. He descended with slightly less confidence than when he had ascended, and started his balancing act all over again, heaving the unwieldy ladder to a relatively level spot beneath the correct window.

There was a knock at Olivia's door, and she started so badly she bumped her head on her window frame. She whirled around, horrified, expecting the worst. Jasper ducked and almost fell from the ladder.

The door opened softly, and Sara's face peeked around the frame.

Olivia almost fainted dead away from relief but suddenly realized the valise was still on her bed, open for all to see.

"Sara! What are you doing up?" she hissed, sitting abruptly on the bed to hide the valise.

"Did you hear that noise?" whispered Sara. "It sounded like someone outside!"

Olivia could hardly speak. "What noise?"

Sara frowned as she caught sight of something behind her aunt's back. "What's that?"

Having secured all the doors and windows on the main floor and finding nothing amiss, Hetty decided it must have been the wind she heard, probably a branch hitting the side of the house. She must have Alec do some pruning for her, she was thinking to herself as she headed for the stairs. Suddenly, however, she heard an unmistakable knocking against the outside wall. No tree limb could make that much noise. Hetty stiffened. It must be an intruder.

Sara's mouth fell open in surprise.

"You're going to what?" she blurted out, a little too loudly.

Olivia put her finger to her lips. "Shhh! Sara! Please!"

Sara's eyes were as big as saucers and her smile spread from ear to ear. "But that's the most romantic thing I ever heard!" She gave her aunt her biggest hug.

"Olivia!" Hetty's voice called up the stairs.

Olivia froze in Sara's embrace and looked to the door in fright, expecting her sister to enter at any moment.

"Olivia!" came the call again.

At the bottom of the stairs, Hetty listened carefully and decided Olivia must have slept through the noise. How typical. An earthquake wouldn't wake her. She decided to investigate the second floor.

Olivia and Sara could hear Hetty's footsteps coming closer and closer. Without a word, Sara grabbed Olivia's valise and threw it and herself under the bed. Olivia stood frozen in a state of shock as the steps grew nearer, and then the door handle turned slowly. Sara grabbed frantically at her ankle to get her to move and Olivia suddenly sprang into action, throwing herself onto the bed and covering herself up to the neck with her eiderdown. Outside, Jasper scrambled halfway down the ladder into the relative safety of the shadows of tree limbs. No one dared to breathe. The bedroom door opened.

Hetty came into the room slowly, her lantern throwing strange, grotesque shapes against the wallpaper. From her hiding place, Sara watched her aunt's slipper-shod feet pass within inches of her nose. She closed her eyes and prayed, and her prayer was answered. The feet turned and went in the other direction, towards the window. Sara held her breath.

Hetty peered out into the darkness of the night. Everything seemed to be in order—the noises had ceased, the silence was disturbed only by the crickets and the cicadas announcing that warm weather was on the way. She closed the sash quietly and crossed the room on tiptoe, glancing at Olivia's sleeping form. At last she went back out into the hall and closed the door behind her.

Letting out a shared sigh of relief, Sara crawled out from under the bed and Olivia threw back the covers and ran to the window.

"Olivia…"

Both Olivia and Sara jumped, but this time the voice was decidedly masculine and came from the trees outside. They threw open the window and leaned out, smiling, as Jasper made his way to the top of the ladder once again. He appeared at the open window, his disembodied head seeming to float in the darkness.

"She's here, Jasper. She's ready," whispered Sara, excitedly.

When Jasper saw Sara, he almost fell off the ladder once again.

Olivia ran to him and grabbed his hands. "It's all right. She knows," whispered Olivia, closing her valise hurriedly.

"Are you sure you want to go through with this?" Jasper asked his bride-to-be as she threw on a shawl and headed for the window.

"Yes," Olivia replied with a sudden, wide smile of happiness, and she kissed him soundly. "Here." She handed Jasper her valise, still looking over her shoulder towards her bedroom door in fear.

Jasper took the valise and started down the ladder, but he had only taken two steps when the suitcase snaps sprang open. He desperately tried to juggle it, but it threw him hopelessly off balance. The ladder slid sideways and Jasper slid with it, disappearing from the window before the horrified eyes of Sara and Olivia. Olivia screamed.

Hearing the screams, Hetty raced outside, armed with a heavy broom.

"Hold on, Olivia. I'm coming!" she called.

As Sara and Olivia watched in disbelief, the valise fell to the ground and intimate garments scattered through the air, landing in the rose-bushes, on the ground and on the unfortunate Jasper's head. Jasper was still clinging desperately to the ladder, but he was fighting a losing battle as it slid farther along the house.

Just as Hetty arrived around the corner of the cottage, the ladder crashed to the ground. Jasper fell through the tree limbs and landed at her feet among the rosebush thorns and the litter of under-things, a pair of bloomers over his head.

Olivia screamed again, and she and Sara disap-peared from the upstairs window, ran from the room and hurtled down the stairs.

Still convinced that the groaning apparition in her rosebushes was an intruder, Hetty lost no time in attacking the culprit. How dare anybody try to sneak into Rose Cottage? Over her dead body would they get away with it! She was whacking the figure unmercifully with her broom when Sara ran around the corner of the house.

"Aunt Hetty! Stop! It's Jasper!" her niece cried frantically.

Hetty stared at Sara and stopped. She whipped the bloomers off the so-called intruder's head and looked at the woebegone Jasper in silent disbelief.

"Jasper Dale!" she exploded. "What in the name of Providence are you doing here?"

Olivia appeared around the corner of the house and immediately dropped to her knees by her groaning fiancé's side. "Jasper? Are you all right?" she cried.

Hetty was slowly putting two and two together. She looked down at the ladder lying on the ground and up to the open window. She picked up one of Olivia's underthings and hastily hid it behind her back. The open, upturned valise among the bushes caught her eye, and a horrified expression came over her face as the penny dropped.

"Olivia King! As I live and breathe. You were about to elo— , elo—" As hard as she tried, she couldn't for the life of her get the word out.

"Elope." Jasper finished the sentence for her.

"Elope," echoed Hetty, in a tone that was more like a croak than her natural speaking voice.

Sara beamed hopefully. "Isn't it romantic?"

Hetty's eyes goggled as she looked at Olivia and Jasper still huddled on the ground together.

"It is despicable!" she raged, and she began hitting Jasper with the broom again with newfound energy. "How dare you even think of tarnishing the King name in such a manner?"

Olivia was on her feet in a second and grabbed the broom away from her sister with surprising strength. "Stop that! Stop it, Hetty! It was my idea!"

Hetty stared at Olivia, hardly comprehending what she had said. "Your idea?" she repeated. "Your idea?" She grabbed the broom back.

Sara held her breath. She had never seen her Aunt Hetty in such a state before.

Hetty stood quite still, gathering her wits. Three faces, white with shock, watched her from the shadows of the garden.

"Well," she continued quietly, giving Jasper and Olivia the evil eye, "it's obvious that neither of you is capable of thinking in a rational manner. So! Jasper Dale!" she said, jabbing at the poor man with the broom handle. "Home!" She turned fiercely to her niece. "Sara Stanley! Bed!" She whirled around and glared at Olivia. Taking her by her arm, she pulled her towards the front door of Rose Cottage. "Olivia! Inside! From now on, I'm in charge!"

Chapter Four

Hetty King, as always, was true to her word. In her mind, Olivia's ridiculous and scandalous attempt at elopement had proven beyond a doubt that she was not capable of organizing anything more important than a bake sale. She vowed that the lovesick couple would be taken in hand, and the morning after that fateful night, she put her pledge into action. Before Sara and Olivia's eyes, she became the surrogate mother of the bride, and all of Olivia's previous wedding plans were swept aside. Gone was the simple outdoor ceremony. The reception was no longer to be a family picnic. Not while Hetty King was in charge!

Before poor Olivia knew what was happening, she found herself being dragged along Avonlea's main street towards the Lawsons' general store, her sister Hetty's arm firmly entwined in her own.

"Hetty, listen to me," she wailed in protest. "I don't need a fancy wedding dress! My blue taffeta or my white suit would be just fine."

Hetty's mouth was set in a firm, thin line. "Since I have gone to the considerable trouble of arranging a proper church wedding, you are also having a proper wedding dress."

Sara sighed as she hurried along behind, trying to keep up. The weather had turned very warm suddenly and a haze seemed to have settled on the village. The very thought of a heavy wedding dress was daunting. But Sara knew very well that if that's what her Aunt Hetty had set her mind on, that's the way things would be.

Hetty had spent the entire morning with Reverend Leonard, bargaining her way into a time slot in an already full schedule of June weddings. She could not fathom why there was a problem. If he had time to perform Olivia and Jasper's wedding before, why did he not have time now?

Finding himself under fire, the poor man protested that leading the vows at an informal outdoor ceremony for twenty minutes or so was quite a different thing from officiating at a full-fledged church wedding. It was only after a very generous donation to the restoration of the church vestry that a two-hour gap in the Reverend's busy schedule was found.

The minute the church had been secured to her satisfaction, Hetty had come to the next item on her newly written list—the wedding dress. Hence the trip to the general store. Hetty had no doubt that, even at this late date, Mrs. Lawson would understand immediately the need for haste in this matter and would be sure to come through for them without hesitation or argument, unlike Reverend Leonard. After all, Mrs. Lawson was a woman.

There were quite a few young ladies of Avonlea tying the knot over the next few weeks, and Mrs. Lawson was up to her ears in orders for wedding dresses. It seemed to her that no one sewed their own dresses any more or inherited them from relations. The trend of the day was to order brand-new ones from the fancy city catalogues. It was good for business—Mrs. Lawson agreed with her husband on that score—but it was she, of course, who had to handle it all, and mothers of brides-to-be could be a very tedious lot. At that very moment an extremely flustered Mrs. Lawson was looking after just such a pair and trying to smooth some very troubled waters.

Mrs. Eulalie Bugle was a large, overbearing woman, and her bride-to-be daughter was, though barely seventeen, even bigger. Cornelia Bugle had just emerged from behind a curtain wearing a wedding dress that was obviously too small for her.

"It won't do up!" wailed Cornelia.

Mrs. Bugle bustled over to her daughter. "Nonsense, Cornelia. Do your corset up tighter," she admonished, and she set about doing just that in front of a very embarrassed Mrs. Lawson.

The bell above the door rang and Hetty, Sara and Olivia entered the store. Sara watched, barely concealing a smile, as Mrs. Bugle tried desperately to tighten her daughter's corset and get the hooks and eyes of the dress to meet at the back, but to no avail. Cornelia, in the meantime, helped herself to a piece of peanut brittle from a nearby jar on the counter.

Thwarted, Mrs. Bugle became righteously indignant. "Well, Mrs. Lawson, this is a fine kettle of fish, isn't it?" she bellowed. "It's plain as plain you took the wrong measurements!"

Mrs. Lawson looked at the woman in astonishment. "I couldn't possibly have done that, Mrs. Bugle. I'm sure of it." She paused, not knowing whether to mention the obvious. "Perhaps Cornelia has gained a little..." She looked pointedly at Cornelia devouring the peanut brittle.

Mrs. Bugle bristled with indignant fury. "I don't want any excuses! What are we gonna do, with the wedding only days away?"

Hetty's ears pricked up. "Really, Mrs. Bugle?" she inquired, sidling over to the woman for the sole purpose of gaining information. Mrs. Bugle was, in her mind, the wrong sort, and under any other circumstances, she would never have passed the time of day with her.

"This Saturday at four," announced the woman proudly. "At the Presbyterian Church, of course. She's marryin' young Hiram Sprockett."

Hetty could barely conceal her amused contempt at the woman's preening. You'd think she was announcing a coronation!

"How charming," she smiled. "My sister Olivia is to be married this Saturday at two."

"That Reverend Leonard is gonna be a busy man," observed Mrs. Bugle as she turned back to Mrs. Lawson. She'd show that high and mighty Hetty King a thing or two. Looking down her nose at her as if she was second class. She deserved better treatment and service. As good as any member of the King family would expect. With this thought firmly lodged in her brain, she turned on the unfortunate Mrs. Lawson.

"Now see here, Mrs. Lawson, I want another dress or my money back."

Before the poor proprietor could reply, Mrs. Bugle picked up the dress catalogue and flipped through it. "Now, that's a peach...a real peach," she said as she stabbed at the open page with a chubby finger. "Isn't it, Corny?" She turned to her daughter and snatched the peanut brittle out of her hand. "Stop that munching!"

Sara inched her way between Mrs. Lawson and Mrs. Bugle to get a better look at the picture Mrs. Bugle was riveted to. Secretly, she was glad that her Aunt Olivia was going to have a real wedding dress and a fancy wedding. There was something fairy-tale-like about a bride with all the trimmings, and she knew her Aunt Olivia would make an especially beautiful one.

Mrs. Lawson fluttered around and tried to turn the page to another design. "Oh. I'm afraid, Mrs. Bugle, that it's the most expensive dress in the book. Peau-de-soie, copied straight from a Paris original, you know. The train is ten feet long."

Sara hid a smile at Mrs. Lawson's pronunciation of peau-de-soie. It came out more like 'Po-ee de Soo'. But whatever material the dress was made of, she couldn't help but admit it was beautiful. In fact, it was one of the most beautiful gowns Sara had ever seen, a confection of creamy ivory silk, sprinkled with tiny seed pearls, with a high, graceful neckline trimmed in lace. The sleeves were tight to the elbows, above which they blossomed into puffs. Sara sighed just looking at it.

"It is pretty, Aunt Olivia," she said, pulling her aunt over to the book. "Come look!"

Hetty struggled to see over their shoulders, not wanting to miss anything.

Olivia took one look at the drawing and protested, "Oh no. It's far too grand for me...besides, Hetty...look at the price..."

Mrs. Bugle raised her eyebrows and gave Hetty a sideways glance. "Nothing is too good for my daughter," she announced.

Hetty caught the note of challenge in Eulalie Bugle's voice and rose to it. "The price is of no account," she said hastily.

"Absolutely..." agreed Mrs. Bugle.

"We'll take it," both women chorused in the same breath.

Olivia was flabbergasted. "Hetty!" she cried, but she was cut off instantly as her sister, who had misread her apprehension as a fear of having the same dress as someone else, whispered in her ear: "Don't worry, Olivia, no one at *her* wedding will be at *our* wedding."

"Make sure you order it in the right size this time," Mrs. Bugle said haughtily to Mrs. Lawson just as the poor woman started to write out the double order. Though she tried not to show it, she was beside herself at the thought of placing it at such a late date—why, the two weddings were less than a week away!

"It will be here on time, of course?" inquired Hetty, reading her thoughts.

"Well, it's awfully short notice, Hetty..." stammered Mrs. Lawson.

"It better be here before the wedding!" bellowed Mrs. Bugle. "Considerin' it was your mistake that put us in this position!"

Mrs. Lawson rolled her eyes in frustration. "I'll do my best Hetty, Mrs. Bugle."

"Please do," replied Hetty primly, pleased that Elvira Lawson had the good sense to address her ahead of this dreadful Bugle woman.

Mrs. Lawson closed the order book with a slam, and Sara was sure she saw her say a little prayer for patience before she picked up her tape measure and, smiling, faced a very forlorn Olivia. "I'll just measure you, shall I?"

"Hmmph! Fat lot of good that seems to do," declared Mrs. Bugle, who nodded her head so vigorously to make her point that her chins wagged.

Mrs. Lawson ignored the woman's snide comment and wrapped the tape measure around Olivia's hips. Olivia was a little taken aback, embarrassed to be measured right there, in front of everybody. To add to her humiliation, her fiancé chose just that moment to enter the store.

Jasper Dale took two steps into the general store and stopped in his tracks as he took in the scene. He smiled instinctively when he saw Olivia. His heart always took a bump whenever he laid eyes on her, but it sank the instant he realized Hetty was also in attendance. He wavered for a moment between retreating and going forward, torn between the desire to talk with Olivia and the fear of having to face Hetty.

A distracted Mrs. Lawson looked up at him, still holding the tape around Olivia's hips. "Can I help you, Jasper?" she called, wishing to heaven her husband was in the store and not upstairs having a nap. When was it her turn to nap? she'd like to know.

Jasper reddened as all the women turned and stared at him. "I…well I, that is…I find…I need a white dress shirt," he stammered.

"I'll be with you in a minute," Mrs. Lawson said tersely, once again silently denouncing her husband for his time away from the counter. She moved the tape to Olivia's bust line.

This was more than Olivia could bear. She felt she had never in her life been more embarrassed and she pushed the tape away.

"Please, Mrs. Lawson. We can do this later," she insisted, her eyes flitting from Jasper to the woman, hoping she would get the hint.

Jasper backed away towards the door. "Well uh, I can...I can...come back another time. You're busy...I can see that..." He smiled and waved a salute to Olivia, who smiled back at him. "Olivia...Mrs. Lawson...Hetty..."

Jasper slowly backed out of the store, almost upsetting a basket of apples in doing so. The women exchanged glances, and Mrs. Lawson proceeded to take the rest of Olivia's measurements.

Jasper stood on the porch of the general store, not quite knowing what to do. The heat wrapped itself around him like a blanket and he mopped his brow. Suddenly the door swung open and shut behind him.

"I'll bet you're sorry you didn't elope."

Jasper turned around to face a half-serious Sara as she plopped herself down on the steps.

"No," said Jasper. "It's only right that Olivia has a proper wedding. I've said that all along." He suddenly thumped his fist into the palm of his hand. "But dang it, Sara, if I can't even get the proper words out in a normal conversation, how am I ever going to get through the ceremony?"

"You'll be fine," said Sara matter-of-factly. "All you have to say is, 'I do'."

Jasper looked down at his feet. "Yes...but...well, there was...uh...something else I'd very much like to say."

"What?" asked Sara, wondering why he was so upset and concerned.

"Well...uh...oh...in my head...I kind of imagined...I'd give a little speech..."

"A speech?" Sara couldn't keep the surprise out of her voice. Never in all the time she had known him had Jasper Dale ever voiced any desire whatsoever to do such a thing.

"A toast...to the bride...to Olivia. I'd like to stand up there in front of everybody and tell Olivia how I feel..." Jasper turned beet-red at the very thought of his proposal.

Sara jumped to her feet, her blue eyes shining. "That's a lovely idea!"

Jasper was suddenly sorry he had said anything. His face fell and he turned to leave. "Yes, but that's all it is. Just an idea. And a silly one at that."

Sara wasn't about to let him get away. She flew off the steps and after him.

"Jasper. You can do it," she said earnestly, taking his arm. "I took elocution lessons in Montreal. And my aunt has coached me in public speaking!"

Sara's aunt was the famous actress, Pigeon Plumtree, who had once graced the village of Avonlea with her presence and talents.

"And Aunt Hetty has a book of speeches," continued Sara in a rush. "I'll pick just the right one and coach you."

Jasper turned around with an almost horrified expression on his face.

"Jasper!" said Sara. "You'll be fine. I'll help you!"

The door of the general store slammed again, and Olivia and Hetty, Mrs. Bugle and Cornelia came out. Jasper saw them coming over Sara's shoulder, and by the time she finished her last sentence, he had hightailed it up the street.

Olivia called to him, but he was already gone.

"My father has booked the ballroom of the White Sands Hotel for my reception," reported Cornelia, between bites of a butter tart.

"Cost us an arm and a leg," added Mrs. Bugle. Let Hetty King put that in her pipe and smoke it, she thought to herself.

Hetty pulled herself up to her full height and looked the woman right in the eye. "The Kings don't believe in the crassness of wedding receptions in public buildings. Family celebrations have always been held at the King farm, you see."

Hetty took Olivia's arm and proceeded down the steps.

Mrs. Bugle glared at her rival. "Well, la-di-da," she called after the King sisters. "Come along, Cornelia." The mother of the bride and her rather sticky daughter put their noses in the air and walked off in the opposite direction.

Olivia couldn't believe her ears. "Hetty, have you spoken to Janet about this?" she asked in an agonized voice.

Hetty looked surprised, as if such a thing had never entered her mind. "No, I have not. Besides, Janet's opinion has nothing to do with it."

With that, she walked off down the road, leaving Sara with her secret and Olivia with a sinking feeling in the pit of her stomach.

Chapter Five

"Are you telling me the reception will be here, in my house?" A horrified Janet King stared at her sister-in-law as if she had lost her senses.

Hetty remained unperturbed. "Only if it rains. If it's sunny it can be outside and it won't inconvenience you in the least."

"Won't inconvenience me? It was one thing to prepare a picnic lunch. I was only too glad to help out. But a reception at the King farm for fifty? With less than a week to prepare? I don't think it's possible."

Hetty sighed and rolled her eyes. "How like you, Janet, to be so negative."

Janet counted to ten, trying desperately to control her temper, but she only got as far as three before she exploded.

"Hetty King, have you lost your mind? How dare you assume that it would be fine with me? I have a houseguest arriving at any moment...I have an infant to care for..."

Hetty couldn't believe the fuss her brother's wife was making. "Do you have any idea the work that goes into organizing something like this?" she asked Janet. How like the woman not to see her side of it.

Eleven-year-old Felix interrupted what would have been a very dangerous situation by running through the hallway and out the front door. "She's here!" he yelled.

"Oh, dear God," mumbled Janet as she looked beyond Felix to the yard. Sure enough, the buggy pulled into the driveway, Alec at the reins, Great-Aunt Eliza beside him. Felicity and Cecily swept down the stairs and past Janet and Hetty, making a huge racket.

"They're here! They're here! Mother, Aunt Eliza's here!"

The door slammed after them.

"Where's the baby, Felicity?" Janet called after her disappearing daughter.

"Asleep!" yelled Felicity over her shoulder.

"Asleep," Janet repeated.

Hetty watched Janet as she wiped her brow, smoothed her apron and prepared to meet her oldest surviving relative. "You know, Janet, if you were better organized, you'd not find yourself in such a constant tizzy about everything!"

Janet glared at her, but further words were made impossible when the sound of a crying baby reached their ears from above. Janet gave Hetty a last, withering look and ran up the stairs to get Daniel. Hetty raised an eyebrow and wondered where this family would be without her? She was the only one with a cool head on her shoulders.

"Good heavens, Alec, thanks to this rickety old thing, I'm black and blue all over," complained Great-Aunt Eliza as Alec helped her down from the buggy. With an ability that never failed to amaze, she had once again managed to alienate him within her first two seconds on King soil.

"I believe that you deliberately looked for every pothole to drive through from that ghastly train station to here," she continued, brushing the dust from her heavy black traveling clothes.

Thirteen-year-old Felicity arrived at Great-Aunt Eliza's side, beaming, tossing her shiny brown curls and looking forward to the usual compliments that people unfailingly paid her.

"Felicity!" declared Aunt Eliza, looking her up and down most severely. "You haven't grown at all!"

Felicity's face fell and she traded looks with her father.

"Oh there you are, my dear!" Eliza waited for Janet to make her way from the house, carrying a fretful Daniel.

"Aunt Eliza," said Janet, giving her great-aunt the best embrace she could manage with a squirming baby in her arms.

Eliza held her at arms length and appraised her with a critical eye. "Janet! Oh my dear, you look positively worn out!"

Janet smiled weakly at this expression of concern. She had actually thought she looked quite well when she'd grabbed a half-second glance at herself that morning, before the demands of daily life took over.

Alec, watching, bit his tongue. "Felix, will you help with the suitcases, please?" he said, with more irritation towards his son than he really felt.

Felix looked surprised at his father's gruff tone but did as he was told and began the grueling task of lifting Great-Aunt Eliza's many pieces of luggage down from the buggy and into the house. He wondered how such a frail little woman could possibly need all these things.

Janet sighed as she watched what would be the beginning of a week tense with petty arguments. She dearly loved her great-aunt, but sometimes she could be just a bit trying. And she certainly brought the worst out in Alec.

Suddenly, she felt something wet and cold against the back of her neck. Janet wiped at it and her hand came away covered in mud. She turned slowly to see a huge dog digging away in her flower garden, sending out showers of earth and greenery behind him.

"Where in the dickens has that dog come from?" she exclaimed. Felix and Felicity shrugged and Cecily looked innocent.

"Get away from there!" Janet passed Daniel to Felicity and gave chase to the dog. "Go on! Go home."

The golden-haired dog ran a little distance away and then sat and stared at her, his tail wagging.

Hetty had sauntered out to the yard after she was sure the initial fuss of the new arrival had run its course. "Eliza. How nice to see you," she said graciously as she took the elderly lady's hand. "Well, at least *you'll* be able to appreciate my plans for the wedding." Hetty led her away around the yard. "Now, tell me what you think. This is where the reception line will form…and the wedding photograph will be taken there, in front of the trees…and this is where I thought we would set up the tables …"

Hetty's voice drifted off and Janet took a deep breath. She took the baby from Felicity and made a beeline for Alec, who was struggling with a huge trunk, trying to shoulder it and carry it to the house.

"Alec!" Janet hissed at him. "You've got to do something. Tell her it's out of the question!"

Alec was thoroughly confused as to what Janet was talking about. Just as he was about to answer civilly, one of the clasps on the trunk snapped open, hitting him squarely on the cheek.

"Janet, I am in no mood. Let's just get this over with as quickly as possible."

"Well, that's all very well for you to say! But I'm the one who has to do everything ..."

Eliza came up to Janet, a smiling Hetty directly behind her. "So, you're going to have the reception here! I think that's a splendid idea."

Alec King dropped the trunk he was holding. "What?"

"Do be careful with my things, Alec." Aunt Eliza tut-tutted and called for Felix to help.

Daniel started to scream and Janet handed him impatiently to Alec . "I was trying to tell you..."

"You know, Alec," said Aunt Eliza, as she perused the King property critically over the rim of her pince-nez, "you should spruce this place up a bit. Maybe the wedding will light a fire under you."

Daniel answered for Alec, breaking into new screams of anger and frustration, wriggling in his father's grasp.

Aunt Eliza took him from Alec with a withering look. "He's teething. Anyone can see that," she said matter-of-factly, as if Janet and Alec didn't have a parental bone between them. She stuck her finger in the baby's mouth and he quieted immediately, contentedly sucking on it.

"Bravo!" said Hetty. Janet looked skyward.

Chapter Six

There wasn't a breath of air moving in the usually cool Rose Cottage. The hot spell had settled in and showed no signs of abating. But Sara didn't mind. She was too excited by her new challenge. Down on her hands and knees in the Rose Cottage parlor, she poured through Hetty's books. The shelf next to the fireplace was full of volumes with some of the strangest titles Sara had ever read. *Etiquette: The Long and the Short of It*; Sara wondered how such a distinction could be made on the subject. *A Brief History of the World* was another one that baffled her. How could the world's history ever be shortened into...she thumbed through the book...ninety-five pages?

Finally, her eye spotted exactly what she had been looking for, a tiny leather book with gold lettering on its spine: *A Guide to Appropriate Toasts and Speeches*. Sara smiled triumphantly and pulled it from its place. She blew the dust from the top of its gilt-edged pages and started to leaf through it.

"What are you up to?"

Sara jumped at the sound of her Aunt Olivia's voice and immediately hid the book in her apron.

"Nothing," she said coyly. "Just something for the wedding."

Olivia sighed and sat down heavily on the sofa. "Ah yes ... the wedding."

"What's wrong, Aunt Olivia?" Sara joined her, but no sooner had she sat down beside her, then Olivia stood up and started to pace restlessly back and forth.

"Oh, I don't know. I'm sure it will all work out. Jasper doesn't seem to mind. In fact, I think he's happy now that it's not at his farm, and it was mainly for him that I wanted to..." She looked towards the door furtively, not wanting to say the word "elope" out loud. "You know. And anyway, Hetty has promised to keep it simple."

As she spoke, Olivia picked up a piece of lined paper from the library table in the middle of the room. It was a list. A guest list. And it wasn't just one page, it was a sheaf!

"Oh! Great Jehoshaphat!" she cried. "It's four pages long, Sara! Hetty!" she called and set off for the kitchen.

❧❧❧

"You don't like it, do you?" asked Olivia quietly.
Jasper turned and faced her. "Like what?"
"The idea of having the wedding here.
All the people…"

❧❧❧

Olivia and Sara threw open the window
and leaned out, smiling, as Jasper made his way
to the top of the ladder.

❧❧❧

Her Aunt Olivia had never looked so beautiful,
thought Sara. A tear rolled down Hetty's cheek as she
listened to Olivia exchange vows with Jasper.

❧❧❧

The entire King clan lined up under the apple tree
to have their photograph taken.

She almost collided with her sister as Hetty entered the parlor from the hall, her face buried in yet another list.

"Hetty King! This is supposed to be a family wedding," began a very agitated Olivia. "I don't even *know* some of these people."

Hetty held her hand up for silence and then rubbed her forehead fretfully with it. "Olivia. Don't start! It took me all day to compile that guest list. You have no idea how difficult it is to do without slighting people right and left. Just be thankful I did it for you."

"But it just isn't what we planned! Jasper wants to keep it simple!" Olivia was trying desperately to keep her voice controlled, but a note of panic rang through loud and clear.

"This is your wedding, Olivia, not Jasper's. Remember that!" said Hetty. "Now, about the flowers," she continued, blind to Olivia's frustration. "There's nothing worth looking at locally, that's for sure. I'll have to send to Charlottetown, I suppose..." She turned decisively and left the room.

"Hetty!" Olivia followed, trying to get her sister's attention.

The minute Sara heard the word "flowers" she joined the parade into the hall.

"Felicity and I are doing the flowers," she said to her aunt's back.

"Don't be silly, Sara," Hetty said with a small chuckle that both Sara and Olivia found extremely irritating.

"But the Queen Anne's Lace!" insisted Sara. "What about all the Queen Anne's Lace Felicity and I found?"

"It can stay in Mrs. Biggins's garden where it belongs," replied Hetty lightly, not realizing the feelings she had trod on as she disappeared through the kitchen door.

Olivia was almost shaking she was so upset. "Oh I give up! Obviously what I want doesn't matter!" She stomped up the stairs.

Hetty poked her nose out from the kitchen door in surprise and looked at Sara as if to say, "What do you suppose has gotten into her?"

Sara glared at Hetty and flounced after Olivia.

"I had hoped for a little cooperation!" Hetty called after the both of them, and then, shaking her head at the load she had to bear, she disappeared back into the kitchen.

Chapter Seven

The weather continued to be unseasonably warm. The almanac for once was wrong, said the farmers, their faith badly shaken in the bible of their trade. It had predicted a rainy, cold June when, in fact, talk at the general store had established that it was the hottest June in twenty years, with no sign of change. The cicadas were buzzing and the flowers were drooping in the King garden.

Janet King felt a little wilted herself. As she kneaded bread dough on the kitchen table, she stared in disbelief at Hetty's four-page list, which Sara held up in front of her. The heat in the kitchen was almost unbearable. Four chickens were roasting in the oven, in preparation for huge amounts of chicken salad for the reception. Janet's hair fell from its pins untidily, and she sighed, wiping flour and perspiration from her forehead.

Sara watched her solemnly. She had not looked forward to this errand, but her Aunt Hetty was busy with more lists and had insisted she go.

"There must be a hundred names on this list!" said Janet in a panic, kneading the bread viciously.

"One hundred and twenty-two," announced Sara with accuracy. "Not counting Olivia and Jasper."

"Alec!" Janet called frantically, but there was no answer. Instead, Aunt Eliza swept into the room.

"I don't know why you're calling for him. As far as I can see, he's never here when you need him, Janet. Besides, I'd be surprised if half those people showed at this late date."

Janet rubbed her hand over her face and tried to collect her thoughts. One hundred and twenty-two people! Even if half didn't show up, there would still be over sixty mouths to feed. And Janet knew in her heart of hearts that it would be a rare person who missed a King wedding. Why, when she and Alec were married, they had invited seventy and entertained ninety.

Baby Daniel cried from his cradle in the kitchen and Janet jumped. "Felicity! The baby," she called, once more to no response. Was there no one in this house to give her any help? "Felicity!" she called more sharply.

Felicity appeared in the doorway of the summer kitchen, stirring batter in a bowl. She looked hot and messy and in a very peevish mood. "Mother, I can't do everything!" she snapped, sticking the spoon in the batter and attempting to hook an errant curl behind her ear. Sara thought that she had never seen Felicity look quite so…normal.

Great-Aunt Eliza rolled her eyes at all the noise and fuss. Such commotion over a simple thing like a baby crying! She lifted Daniel out of the crib and rocked him slowly in her arms. He instantly stopped crying. Janet knew in her heart she should be grateful, but her mothering instincts came to the fore and she felt more than just a small twinge of jealousy and resentment.

Felicity looked at Sara, all calm and cool in her fresh summer dress, her hair neatly pulled back in a matching silk ribbon, and felt her own kind of resentment. "You and Aunt Hetty could make yourselves far more useful by doing something other than sitting around and making lists," she snapped.

"Felicity!" her mother admonished, but Sara could see that her aunt wished she'd said the very same thing.

Felicity walked back into the summer kitchen in a huff.

Sara sighed in frustration. She hated being caught in the middle like this, and she didn't blame them for feeling the way they did. If she could only explain that the whole thing was out of her and Olivia's hands. "Felicity!" she called to her cousin as she followed her through the door.

Janet took another look at the list and threw it on the table.

"If you don't mind, Janet, I'd love a cup of tea," chirped Aunt Eliza, still rocking the now happy baby. "I don't know why, but my bones are always so chilled in this house."

Janet gritted her teeth and wiped perspiration from her brow. "It's eighty-five degrees outside, Aunt Eliza," she said briskly.

Alec walked in from the yard, sweaty and dirty, and went straight for the sink to wash up. "I'm hungry," he remarked with gusto, and he instantly felt two pairs of eyes boring into him.

Aunt Eliza cleared her throat delicately. "Alec, I was out for a wee stroll after my morning tea and I couldn't help but notice that old plow behind the barn. It is an eyesore. You've got to move it before the wedding," she announced. Satisfied that she had won Alec's full attention, she turned back to Janet and continued her previous conversation. "You don't feel the cold the way I do," she observed peevishly as Janet fanned herself with a dishcloth.

Alec didn't quite know whether he was supposed to reply to the order he had just been given or not. He was hot. He was tired. He had just cut all the grass around the driveway because earlier that morning Janet had complained of it being unsightly. And, over the last day or so, Alec had listened to about enough of Aunt Eliza to last him a lifetime. He dried his hands and hung up the towel, trying to control the temper he felt rising. It was no use. He turned to the woman who sat, the picture of innocence, looking down at his baby son, cooing like a small bird. His words stuck in his throat. Instead, he swung around to face Janet.

"Look," he sputtered, "if she wants the plow moved…she's got two arms!"

"Alec King!" Janet cried, shocked at her husband's rudeness. What would her aunt think?

She needn't have worried. Alec's words had gone over Aunt Eliza's head completely and she continued on her former train of thought.

"Oh, Janet." The elderly lady shook her head wisely. "You'll be old soon, too, one of these days. Then you'll find out."

Janet felt she had aged twenty years in the last half hour. She waved the guest list at Alec, shoving it under his nose. "Look at this! It's getting totally out of hand!"

"Well then why don't you just tell Hetty?" Alec snapped at her.

Janet looked at him, her eyes wide with incredulity. "Me? She's your sister."

"It's your family wedding, Alec," Aunt Eliza piped up. "Why should Janet bear the brunt, with a six-month-old baby in the bargain?"

"For once in your life, Eliza, stay out of this!" The words left Alec's mouth before he had a chance to stop them.

"Don't you talk to my aunt like that!" Janet's voice cracked in the dangerous way Alec recognized as belonging to the stage just before tears.

He was about to apologize when the kitchen

screen door opened and slammed shut and a huge, filthy, golden dog ran through the kitchen tracking mud, with Cecily in hot pursuit.

"No! Stop! Come back!" Cecily called in vain, throwing herself at the dog and missing him just as he found his way into the summer kitchen.

This was the last straw for Janet. "Cecily King! Keep that dog outside or I will not promise its safety," she shrieked.

Cecily beamed with hope. "Does that mean we can keep him?"

"No," Alec answered sharply, "it doesn't mean any such thing, young lady. Now do as you're told!" Alec hardly ever raised his voice to his children, but when he did, they listened. The dog turned and growled at him, and Cecily's face crumpled. She started to cry as she dragged the dog out the door by the scruff of the neck.

"There was no need to shout at her!" said Janet, her voice breaking again. She buried her face in her hankie and stomped up the back stairs. Alec threw down the offending list and, slamming the door behind him, headed towards the barn.

Aunt Eliza raised a delicately shaped eyebrow as she sat rocking the baby.

"I never did get my tea, did I?" she said to Daniel, who gurgled at her and smiled.

Chapter Eight

Later that week, Sara kept a secret appointment with Jasper Dale. They were probably the only two inhabitants of Avonlea who were not suffering the discomfort of the heat wave as they sat in an idyllic spot beside the stream that ran through the Dale farm, with their feet dangling in its cool, rushing water. Jasper, however, was suffering from another type of discomfort, for if a passerby had looked closely, they would have been amazed to see that Jasper's mouth was full of marbles. He was therefore, understandably, having great difficulty talking.

"Sally...sells...seashells..." he attempted valiantly. "Sara, I can't talk with these...things in my mouth," he muttered, almost unintelligibly.

"If it worked for Demosthenes, it will work for you," declared Sara. "Try it again."

It crossed Jasper's mind that Sara was sounding dangerously like her Aunt Hetty, but he didn't want to disappoint her.

"Sally sells...seashells...by the seashore..." he mumbled, almost swallowing a cat's-eye.

Sara was jubilant. "You see? That's much better. My elocution teacher swore by this exercise. It cured Demosthenes of his stutter."

Jasper nodded and spit the whole mouthful of offending marbles into his hankerchief.

But Sara had not finished with him. "Let's go over the speech. I think it's a perfectly beautiful one, don't you?" she asked, thrusting the little leather book at him, open to the appropriate page.

Jasper scanned the lines in front of him. "Well, yes ..." he conceded, again not wanting to hurt Sara's feelings. "But it's a bit..." he searched for the right word, "fervent," he concluded.

Sara wasn't quite sure what he meant by the word "fervent," but she did know that time was running out, and Jasper had a long way to go.

"Just try it," she said, a smile of encouragement on her face.

Jasper obediently took the book and began reading in a halting manner. "'To my b-b-bride. How can I describe...the m-m-many ways...I love...thee. My l-l-l-love, my life...my only...r-r-reason for living...I toast thee for thy innocence, thy t-t-t-trust and thy...undying devotion....My wife, my heaven-s-s-s- sent...dove of peace...'"

Sara started to recite it along with Jasper, hoping it would help cure him of his stuttering. She began to wonder if it really was possible to get him ready in time for the wedding.

As the "big day" grew ever closer, Sara wasn't the only one who was worried about hitches. The temperature and the tension continued to mount and reached a head the very day before the joyous occasion. And poor Mrs. Lawson found herself in the center of a crisis once again.

"Do you realize the wedding is tomorrow, Elvira?" asked Hetty King in an ominous voice. "What do you suppose you're going to do about it?"

Mrs. Bugle and her daughter bustled their way into the general store and caught the gist of what Hetty was getting at.

"Do you mean to say the dresses aren't here yet?" the woman demanded harshly.

Hetty turned to her and said bluntly, "Olivia's dress isn't here. The wedding is tomorrow!"

Cornelia immediately started to cry and snuffle in a noisy, gulping fashion.

"Hush, Cornelia!" her mother commanded, completely losing any semblance of proper decorum. Cornelia hushed.

Mrs. Lawson wished she had never got out of bed that morning. "Please, ladies, I did my very best, but—" She didn't get a chance to finish.

Mrs. Bugle looked down at the poor woman, her face blotchy as her blood pressure rose. "If those dresses aren't here first thing tomorrow morning, Elvira Lawson, I will throw a blue fit!!!"

"How sensible," muttered Hetty. She raised an eyebrow slightly but nodded in agreement with

Mrs. Bugle, the first and only time they would ever join forces.

"If Olivia's dress isn't here by eleven o'clock tomorrow morning, the Kings will take their business elsewhere from here on in, Elvira, even if it means driving to Markdale for a bag of flour."

"The Bugles will do the same," thundered Mrs. Bugle, not to be outdone.

Mrs. Lawson took a deep breath. "I promise you that the dresses will be here by eleven o'clock tomorrow morning, even if my husband has to drive to Charlottetown to get them."

Chapter Nine

The heat hung like a blanket over Avonlea. There was no respite from the humidity, even after the sun had gone down. Windows and doors were left open in the hope that even a small breeze from the sea would stir the air. But all was still. Not a breath was moving, and the frogs and the cicadas chorused their approval.

The eve of her wedding found Olivia King pacing back and forth in the Rose Cottage kitchen. Brides were supposed to be nervous, but she was approaching a state of apoplexy. Unperturbed, Hetty sat at the big polished wood table, her brows knit with concentration as she drew up a seating arrangement for the reception. Olivia paused for a moment and dared to look at it over her sister's shoulder.

Hetty sighed in frustration. "Goodness knows where to put Eliza. She isn't even related to the Kings and there isn't a Ward who will speak to her, except Janet, and I've already put her at the head table."

"Hetty, I didn't want a head table," declared Olivia in a pitiful voice, her emotions completely frazzled by the events of the past week.

Hetty looked at Olivia and shook her head in disgust. "There's no pleasing you, is there?"

Sara entered the kitchen to help herself to a piece of bread and butter, but the atmosphere was so thick with humidity and tension, she could have cut it with the bread knife.

"I just don't like the idea of sitting apart...I just don't like people staring at us..." Olivia began quietly. "I wanted a simple picnic buffet so that we could...mingle with our guests."

"Mingle!" Hetty laughed outright. "With a ten-foot train trailing along in the dirt?"

"I didn't want a ten-foot train," Olivia cried sharply, her bottled-up feelings threatening to break loose at any second. "And with any luck at all it won't arrive!"

Sara stood still, the slice of bread near her mouth in suspended animation.

Hetty threw her latest plan on the table. "Oh, now that's gratitude for you! I go to all this trouble...bending over backwards..."

"Nobody asked you to, Hetty, for heaven's sake!" cried Olivia, and fighting back tears of frustration, she turned her back on her sister.

Sara stepped forward from the counter. "Stop shouting," she begged. "Both of you. Please...!"

"And I suppose I should have let you run off into the night like a pair of ... gypsies!" Hetty spat out the word as if it tasted like poison. "I wanted you to have the kind of wedding you could be proud of!"

"No! Oh no! You did not!" Olivia retorted, spinning around to look at Hetty with angry tears in her eyes. "You wanted a wedding that *you* would be proud of, Hetty King! Well, whose wedding is this anyway, mine or yours?"

Sara swallowed hard. There was no going back now. Her Aunt Olivia had mouthed what Sara knew had been in her heart all week long, and a huge silence reigned.

Hetty turned her back on her sister and busied herself immediately at the counter. "What a ridiculous question, Olivia," she said quietly, her tone brittle with emotion.

But Olivia wasn't to be stopped, and her voice rose. "The only good thing about this whole business is that it will soon be over with and I'll be able to move away from your constant interfering!"

Hetty's back stiffened and she stood stunned and hurt. Olivia was so angry she couldn't apologize, even though she knew she had gone one step too far. Instead, she escaped, stomping out of the room. The front door slammed.

Hetty turned desperately to her niece, imploring her to understand.

"You've spoiled everything!" cried Sara, who, by this time, was close to tears herself, so upset was she with Hetty for causing Olivia's unhappiness.

"It's just a case of bride-to-be jitters, that's all," Hetty mumbled. "She'll come to her senses."

But Sara didn't reply. She ran out the back door. Hetty stood alone in shocked silence, stunned that her Sara had actually taken Olivia's side.

The faint light of a lantern glowed from the main-floor windows of the Dale farmhouse. Inside, Jasper was pacing. He held a crumpled piece of paper in his hand. "'My love...my life... my only reason for...living.'" He stopped and peered once more at the words on the page and frowned. "'I toast thee for thy innocence, thy trust and thy undying devotion...my wife...my heaven-sent dove of...peace...'"

A sharp knock at the door made him drop the

paper in surprise. He scooped it up and stood quite still. Who could it be at this time of night? he wondered. The knock sounded again, this time harder, and he dodged through the piles of books and papers scattered about the room to make it to his front door.

To his intense surprise, Olivia stood there.

"Jasper!" she cried.

"Olivia...what...?" he managed to utter before she collapsed on his shoulder sobbing, much to his acute embarrassment. He tried desperately to stuff the piece of paper into his vest pocket at the same time as he held her up and patted her awkwardly on the back. Olivia finally calmed down enough to speak.

"Oh Jasper!" she gasped. "I can't go through with this...I can't."

For one brief but terrible moment, Jasper was convinced his worst nightmare had come true. She was here to break her engagement with him, cancel the wedding, she didn't love him after all.... But the next word that tumbled from Olivia's lips was "Hetty," and he immediately understood the true source of her obvious distress.

"Hetty...is so..." she began, but the sobbing took over again.

"There, there," said Jasper, patting her back once more.

Olivia looked up, her big brown eyes brimming with tears. "Why don't we just drive into

Charlottetown, right now, tonight, and have a justice of the peace marry us?"

Jasper could barely find his voice. "Oh now, Olivia…" he got out, wondering what he was ever going to do about this unforeseen crisis.

"You agreed before!" insisted Olivia.

"Only because I thought it would make you happy," Jasper said quietly.

"But I was doing it for you!" she sobbed, thinking again what a miracle it was that she was lucky enough to have found him.

"I will be fine," he soothed. "Don't worry about me."

Olivia looked at him pleadingly. "Then let's just go, now…" The minute she said it, her forehead creased with concern and she started to pace in small, agitated circles. "Oh, I can't do that either…what would Janet ever say? After preparing all that food? She'd never forgive me!" She turned and threw herself at her fiancé. "Oh Jasper, I just don't know what to do! I tried so hard to keep everything simple and it's just completely out of control!"

Jasper took her gently by the arm and sat her down. "Olivia, tomorrow is just one day in the rest of our lives. A very…long day most likely, but still, only one. We'll get through it."

Olivia looked up at him, feeling for the first

time in the entire week that someone cared for her and was looking out for her. "Do you think so?" she asked.

"Yes," replied Jasper firmly, and he kissed her on the forehead.

"I'm just so afraid that you'll hate it. She even has us sitting at a head table…" She bit her bottom lip and waited for Jasper's reaction.

"Oh!" Jasper gulped. "Well, it will be…fine… nice view…"

Olivia felt the wild desire to laugh, and she gazed at him thankfully, a smile lighting up her face.

"I love you…" was all she could say.

"I love you, too," replied Jasper, and he kissed her self-consciously, almost as if someone might be looking through his window. "Now," he said decisively, loosening his collar, "I'll walk you home."

The mood was broken abruptly. Olivia leapt to her feet and stood with her eyes blazing, her mouth set in a stubborn line.

"No! I will not spend another night under the same roof with that woman!"

Jasper was completely unnerved. "Oh! Well, n-n-now…" he stuttered nervously, his face reddening. "I…umm…I don't think you should stay here…it might not look…well…what I mean is…"

Olivia was adamant. "I am not going back to Rose Cottage!"

"You aren't?" Jasper squeaked, and an awkward silence fell as he looked desperately around the room, as if the answer to this dilemma might be written on the walls if only he looked hard enough. Inspiration came from out of the blue. "Well, what about King Farm? You could stay there!"

To his immense relief, Olivia nodded thoughtfully, considering this possibility. "Janet wouldn't mind, would she?"

Jasper nodded his agreement vigorously.

"She's sure to understand…" continued Olivia, and she smiled hopefully at Jasper.

Jasper smiled back and they hugged, both very much relieved that the crisis had passed. If they had known how many more were yet to come, neither of them would have relaxed quite so much.

Chapter Ten

Janet King came slowly down the back stairs, obviously hot and worn out. It was like a furnace upstairs, and the baby had taken much longer than usual to settle. She hated to admit it, but Aunt Eliza had been right. One tiny little white tooth had broken through, and the poor little thing had been miserable all evening. She reached the kitchen and looked around at her afternoon's work: stacks of wrapped sandwiches, bowls of salads, platters of tiny tarts and sweets, all still to be put away in the cool fruit cellar. Her gaze fell in dismay at the dirty dinner dishes, lying undone by the sink. She fought the ridiculous urge to just sit down and have a good cry, but Alec chose that moment to come in from the yard, and her sense of the injustice of it all took aim at him.

"And where have you been?" she asked, her voice coldly accusing.

Alec looked up from taking off his muddy work boots, his face streaked with sweat. "I have been out moving that blasted plow. I just hope it makes your Great-Aunt Eliza happy."

Janet turned her back on him and started vigorously pumping water to heat for the dishes.

Alec took a deep breath, regretting his tone of voice. He valiantly tried to make conversation.

"Are the children in bed?"

"Yes they are," replied Janet without looking at him. "No thanks to you."

Somehow, this wasn't the conversation Alec had had in mind. "I can't be everywhere at once," he growled.

"That's funny," snapped Janet. "I have to be!"

She whisked the water off the stove and started pouring it on the dishes. She'd forgotten there was no fire lit. It was still stone cold, but she didn't care.

"Now Janet, let's just stop this…" Alec pleaded and moved forward to help his wife.

From the top of the back stairway came Aunt Eliza's quavering, high-pitched voice.

"Janet, could you be a dear and switch my mattress with Felicity's? I can't abide horsehair mattresses. My back, you know."

Janet gripped the side of the sink and begged inwardly for mercy.

"I tried to do it, Mother," called Felicity, "but it's too heavy."

Janet moved heavily to the bottom of the stairs. "Please keep your voices down. I just got the baby settled. Why don't you two simply switch beds?"

Eliza looked imperiously down at Janet as if she had suggested she stand on her head for the remainder of the night. "Oh, I couldn't possibly. Hers is much too close to the window…with my arthritis!"

As Janet started upstairs, there was a knock at the front door.

"You answer it!" she snapped, still not looking at her husband.

Alec sighed and left the kitchen. He crossed the hall, wondering how in heaven's name he would get through the next few days. He opened the door and found himself looking down at a very forlorn Sara Stanley.

"Sara, what are you doing out so late?" he demanded, looking at her distraught face.

"I want to stay here," said Sara simply as she walked by him into the hall.

"You what?" said Alec, but he was interrupted by yet another knock at the door.

He opened it to find Jasper and Olivia standing there.

"What the...?" he began, but Olivia threw herself at her older brother and started to cry.

"Hello, Alec," said Jasper, suffering from acute embarrassment.

Janet heard the commotion and came flying down the stairs.

"Olivia, dear. Whatever is the matter?" she cried. "Sara, darling. Tell me..."

Olivia left a dazed Alec and allowed herself to be gathered into Janet's arms.

"Oh Janet," she sobbed. "It's Hetty! I just can't stay there another minute. She's being so horrible!"

Of all people, Janet King knew just how horrible her sister-in-law could be, and she was filled immediately with sympathy for Olivia.

"Oh there, there," she crooned, holding Olivia tightly. "I know. I know. You just come right upstairs...you too, darling." She took Sara under her other wing and led them both away. "Now both of you must stay here. I wouldn't think of sending you back to Rose Cottage."

"Thank you," Olivia gasped before another bout of tears took over.

"Hetty has gone too far!" announced Janet, and she threw a meaningful look over her shoulder to her husband.

Left on their own in the hall, Alec and Jasper exchanged beleaguered looks. The chatter of women's voices drifted down from upstairs as Aunt Eliza, Cecily and Felicity joined forces with the others. The men had been relegated to the sidelines, ignored, as if they didn't exist. Alec motioned to the porch and Jasper gladly followed him.

It was as hot as midday outside. Both men stood looking out into the darkness, rocking back and forth on their heels. After an embarrassed silence, Alec took out his pipe. Jasper started to whistle nervously, but it sounded so out of place that he ceased after the first out-of-tune phrase.

"Well," he said finally, "tomorrow's the day."

"Yeah. It sure is," replied Alec, inhaling deeply on his pipe.

"Yup...yup..." Jasper rocked some more.

Silence fell once again upon the pair. Alec stole a sideways glance at Jasper and realized that the man was rigid with tension.

"Do you have the ring?" he asked, trying to put Jasper at his ease.

Jasper thought for a moment and then nodded. "Yes. Yes, I do."

"Since Felix is the ring-bearer, maybe I should pick it up in the morning," suggested Alec. "I'll make sure it gets to the church."

Jasper nodded in agreement. "Good. Good plan. I tend to forget things...especially...when..." He took a deep breath and shook his head.

Alec smiled. "You're not nervous are you, Jasper?"

"Me? Oh no." Jasper paused. "Some. It's a big step."

"One of the biggest." Alec took his pipe out of his mouth, realizing for the first time that there was absolutely no tobacco in it.

"I sincerely hope that Olivia and I can be as happy as you and Janet," said Jasper quietly.

Alec raised an eyebrow. If only Jasper knew how their marriage had fared over the past few days! "Oh...well. I'm sure you will be. Even when the honeymoon bliss is over."

The word "honeymoon" caused Jasper to break out in a cold sweat, even though the temperature was still well into the eighties. He stole a glance at Alec. He was a married man, he reminded himself. "Well, actually..." he began cautiously. "It's the honeymoon part of it that has me a little worried."

Alec slapped him on the back. "Oh, come on man. Olivia's a bit high-strung, I know she's bound to be a little nervous, but…"

Jasper cleared his throat nervously. "Oh, I'm sure…Olivia will be fine…it's uh…"

Alec looked at his future brother-in-law and understood what he was getting at. "Jasper," he said, "you're going to be fine, too."

Jasper looked at Alec thankfully and took a deep breath.

"Tomorrow's the day…" he said.

Alec smiled. "You'd better go home and get some sleep."

"Yup. That's a good idea." Jasper held out his hand and Alec shook it warmly. The groom-to-be nodded awkwardly, backed off the steps and headed down the drive.

"See you in church," Alec called after him.

"Yup! Good night, Alec," Jasper called. He waved quickly, and then stuck his hands in his pockets and disappeared into the shadows of the apple trees that lined the road.

Alec took a deep breath, tapped his pipe against the wall out of habit, even though nothing came out of it, and stepped back into the house.

Chapter Eleven

Alec found to his surprise that all was quiet in the King household. He couldn't help but breathe a sigh of relief as he walked around blowing out the lamps. He entered the kitchen and finished the dishes for Janet. Satisfied that he had done something, at least, to help her, he surveyed the tidy room and climbed the back stairs.

It always gave Alec a pleasant, contented feeling whenever he walked by the bedroom doors of his children. He could hear their quiet breathing, the occasional rustle of blankets, and at those moments he was filled with the knowledge that all was safe and right with his world.

He tiptoed into the room that he and Janet had shared ever since their wedding day. More years had passed than he cared to remember, but talking with Jasper had brought it all back to him. He smiled down at his wife, her face peaceful and youthful as she slept, free from all the cares and woes that had plagued her throughout the week. Alec felt a sudden pang of regret that he had not kept his word. He hadn't behaved himself. He had let Eliza get under his skin, just as he had vowed he wouldn't. Janet was right to have been angry with him, and he promised himself that he would make it up to her.

He took off his shirt and his pants and sat on the side of the bed in his long johns. He pulled down the covers and made a move to lie down, but then he was so startled he almost cried aloud. There, with her head on his pillow, on his side of the bed, was Great-Aunt Eliza, her mouth open wide, snoring contentedly. Alec grabbed his pants and bolted out of the room.

Leaning against the door, he regained his equilibrium and decided on a course of action.

He opened bedroom door after bedroom door in search of a place to sleep. Felicity and Cecily were sharing their room with Sara. Olivia was asleep in Felix's room with the baby.

Alec stormed downstairs, his conciliatory mood of merely moments before swept aside.

He headed for the parlor only to find the couch occupied by a sleeping Felix.

"For crying out loud!" he exclaimed, and he headed back into the front hall in disgust, mistakenly slamming the parlor door behind him.

Janet appeared at the top of the stairs.

"Shh! You'll wake the baby," she said crossly. "What are you doing wandering around in the middle of the night?"

"I have been looking for a place to bloody sleep," retorted Alec in a loud whisper as he made his way up the stairs. He pointed towards their bedroom door. "What is she doing in there?"

"Olivia's in her bed," replied Janet.

"Where am I supposed to sleep?" hissed Alec.

In the next room, the baby began to cry.

"Now look what you've done!" Janet rolled her eyes in exasperation.

"Every bed in this place is full. I mean, it's a fine state of affairs when a man can't find a place to sleep in his own house!"

Janet's eyes flashed with anger. As if it was *her* fault that their house was full of unexpected guests. How like a man to think only of himself!

"Why don't you go sleep at Rose Cottage?" she snapped. "There's plenty of room there!" Janet turned on her heel and, with the face of a martyr, stormed off to calm Daniel.

A furious Alec stomped down the stairs and into the kitchen. He threw open the back door and almost tripped over the huge golden dog pushing by him on his way in. Alec watched in disbelief as the animal trotted straight for the kitchen couch, jumped up on it and made himself comfortable. Once settled, he turned to Alec and, panting, watched him with great, soulful, brown eyes.

"So you've moved in too, have you?" exclaimed Alec. "Why not? Everyone else has!" With that, he marched through the door, slamming it behind him, and disappeared into the night.

Alec was surprised to see the lights still on at Rose Cottage. He was relieved. At least he wouldn't have to wake Hetty up. He knocked on the door lightly and waited. There was no answer. He tried the door and it opened.

"Hetty!" he called.

The hall was empty and Alec ventured in. "Hetty! Are you here?" he called again as he entered the parlor. As he passed, Alec tested the hard sofa with his hand, grimaced and went back into the hall. Suddenly he heard the unmistakable sound of crying coming from somewhere above.

He took the stairs two at a time and, walking towards the sound, he came to Olivia's bedroom door. It was slightly ajar, and he could see Hetty sitting on the bed among Olivia's packed things. Her back was to Alec and her shoulders were shaking with sobs.

"Hetty?" he said quietly.

Hetty whirled around, startled, not wanting her brother to see that she had been crying. She fiercely wiped her cheeks and eyes with a hankie.

"Alec. What are you doing here?"

Alec attempted a smile. "There's no room at the inn. I wondered if I could bunk in here tonight?"

Hetty turned away, still wiping her eyes. "Yes. Of course you can," she replied, her voice unsteady. "There's lots of empty rooms." She started to cry once again, in spite of herself.

Alec walked slowly towards her, awkward in this unfamiliar situation. His oldest sister had never cried easily. "Oh, now Hetty," he said, as he put a tentative hand on her shoulder

"It's all right," sobbed Hetty. "It's all my own fault. I did everything I swore I would never do. But I couldn't stand by and watch her life get off to such a bad start. My own sister, the only one I have left…and…now I've lost her too…" Her voice trailed off and was smothered in the handkerchief that she pressed to her face.

Alec sat down beside her and patted her back, trying to make sense out of what she was saying. "You haven't lost her," he finally said, quietly. "You haven't lost Olivia. She cares too much about you."

Hetty turned her face away from him.

"It feels like…losing a child. Olivia's been more like a daughter to me…than a sister. My life will be so empty."

Fresh tears accompanied this confession, and Alec was moved to hug her. Without thinking, he found himself rocking Hetty back and forth as he would one of his children.

"I know it won't be the same," he said. "But you can take it from a father who knows, you'll have your hands full with Sara." He patted her back once again, and the sobs began to lessen. "Hetty, everything is going to be fine." He held her out at arm's length and she scrambled to compose her face, dabbing at her eyes with the now drenched hankie.

"Just come over tomorrow, what's one more person in that house?" he added wryly, smiling at her. "You help Olivia get ready, and everyone will forget this ever happened."

Hetty looked at him gratefully and took a deep breath.

"Now, I'm going to get some sleep." Alec got up and walked to the door.

"Thank you, Alec," Hetty's voice followed him. "You can use Sara's room." Her voice caught as she remembered that Sara, too, had turned against her.

Alec gave her a comforting wink. "Good night, Hetty."

Chapter Twelve

Olivia's wedding day dawned with beautiful sunshine and a thermostat reading of eighty-six degrees Fahrenheit—in the shade. Alec was up bright and early at Rose Cottage. Sara's bed had proved much too short for him and he had passed a very restless night.

He arrived at the King Farm to find Sara herself awake and sitting on the porch waiting for him. She was intent on being at the general store the minute it opened, despite Olivia's warning that Mrs. Lawson had promised the dress for eleven o'clock.

Alec was secretly pleased to have something to do that would be helpful to the cause but at the same time keep him out of the house. He remembered his promise to Jasper as well and decided to pick up the ring on their way home.

The town was quite deserted when Alec and Sara pulled up to the general store. Sara hopped down from the buggy and, grinning at her Uncle Alec, held up two sets of crossed fingers.

A triumphant Mrs. Lawson rushed to the back of the store the minute she saw who her first customer was.

"Oh Sara! It's here," she called.

Sara sighed with relief and pleasure. "That's wonderful, Mrs. Lawson!"

The bell rang almost immediately and Mrs. Bugle sailed in to pick up her daughter's dress.

"I'll get yours for you too, Mrs. Bugle!" called Mrs. Lawson gaily.

"It's here?" the woman trumpeted. "Well hallelujah!"

Mrs. Lawson hurried to the counter with two

large white boxes and handed one to Sara and the other to Mrs. Bugle.

"There you are, Sara," she said, giving her hand a squeeze. "Tell Olivia to wear it in good health."

"I will," Sara smiled.

Mrs. Bugle leaned over the counter. "My Cornelia will be lucky to have good health," she whispered to Mrs. Lawson in an undertone, once more a friend and confidante. "Do you have any stomach powder, Mrs. Lawson? Plain nerves is all. She can't keep anything down."

Sara was in a hurry to go. "Thank you again, Mrs. Lawson," she called. "See you at the wedding!"

She raced out of the store and ran to the buggy, waving the box. Alec made a victory sign and they drove away to perform their next errand.

Things were not running quite as smoothly at the King farm. Janet was frazzled. Her hair hung around her face, strands sticking to her cheeks in the heat. She hadn't had a moment to herself to do it up properly. Her apron was covered in flour and stains, and she was attempting to put the finishing touches on the wedding cake after what seemed like a morning of endless interruptions.

Olivia paced fretfully back and forth, every once in a while peering out the window. Great-Aunt Eliza sat in great state nibbling on a cucumber sandwich Janet had been called upon to make.

"Well, Olivia, you'll be a married woman before the day is out," Eliza began. "I do hope it isn't a case of marry in haste, repent at leisure."

Olivia turned and looked at the woman, not quite sure how to respond to this, but Eliza had turned her attention and concern to Janet. She frowned delicately as she took stock of her appearance.

"Janet, dear," she purred, "you're not even dressed. We have to leave in a little more than two hours, you know."

Janet bit her tongue. She knew only too well when they had to leave, and the last thing she wanted was to be reminded of it.

"Oh my goodness," burst out Olivia. "Will that dress ever arrive?" She fled from the room in a complete state and ran up the stairs.

Cecily wandered through the kitchen bouncing a ball, dressed for the wedding in her best clothes. The ball got away from her and landed on the table, narrowly missing the cake.

Janet closed her eyes. "Cecily, I'm not going to tell you again. If you want to play ball, go outside! You're only in the way here."

A downcast Cecily went towards the door.

"And don't get dirty in those good clothes!" her mother called after her.

The door slammed its answer and Janet went back to concentrating on decorating the cake. Felicity made her entrance into the kitchen, twirling around to show off her new dress. She stopped and looked at her mother with a shocked expression.

"Mother! We don't have much time, you know. When are you going to change?"

Janet didn't trust herself to answer her daughter and continued to decorate the cake, placing a delicate yellow rose on its top layer.

Outside, wicker tables and chairs covered the green lawn. All the tables were beautifully set with china and crystal. The buggy pulled into the yard, and Alec and Sara watched a woebegone Cecily walking towards the barn. Sara promised herself she would play with Cecily later, but first she had an important errand to complete. She ran up the stairs of the porch with the white dress box.

"Aunt Olivia! Your dress is here!" she called as she disappeared into the house.

Alec entered a little more sedately. He and Janet had still not exchanged two words since the night before, and he was treading lightly.

Janet was finishing the last curlicue of icing when Alec entered the kitchen. He handed her the ring and she took it, still not choosing to speak to him.

"Felix! Come down, dear," she called, and Felix dawdled into the room, a scowl on his face. He was sweating in his suit, prying at his starched collar.

"Do I have to wear this collar? It's the hottest day in the whole year. I'm going to suffocate."

"Stand still," was all Janet said, needle and thread in hand. "I'm going to sew this ring into your pocket so you won't lose it."

Felix pulled away in disgust. "I'm not gonna lose it. What do you think I am, a baby or something?"

"All right. All right." Janet gave in and handed him the ring, which he immediately stuffed into his left pocket. "Here's a hankie," she said, and she put it in his other pocket.

"I don't need no dumb hankie," he growled, scowling at his mother, and he promptly tried to remove it.

"Felix! Leave it!" Janet commanded shrilly, and the matter was settled.

In the meantime, Cecily took refuge in the barn, where she knew someone would be glad to see her.

"Here puppy, puppy," she called into the darkness. There was no answering bark, no great furry beast galloping towards her. Cecily frowned and called again. This time, she could hear a faint whining near the chicken coop and followed it. She was horrified to find that her "puppy" was caught under one of the outside walls of the barn. He had dug himself halfway out and got stuck.

"Look at you!" cried Cecily. Grabbing a shovel, she began to dig him out, paying no attention whatsoever to the state of her good clothes. "You're a real digger aren't you?" she said as she labored. "That's what I'll call you: Digger!"

The minute Digger was free, he raced out from under the barn wall towards the house, Cecily following in frantic pursuit.

Janet carefully placed another beribboned yellow rose on the very top layer of the wedding cake and took a moment to stand back and admire her handiwork. It was four layers high, made of rich fruitcake covered in meticulously fluted white icing. She had to admit, it was beautiful. Olivia would be thrilled. Maybe all this work would be worth it in the end.

She proudly carried the cake from the counter to the table and then went to the sink to wash her hands. The front door opened and closed as Felix went out to join his father at the buggy. The next thing she knew, a horrified Felicity was standing on the back stairs and pointing mutely to the table.

"Mother!" She could barely get the word out.

Janet turned to find the huge golden dog licking the bottom layer of her precious cake, his rough tongue taking the icing with it.

Janet stood frozen in a state of shock and then grabbed the nearest weapon she could get her hands on—the kitchen broom. The dog took one look at the broom and was out of the room before Janet could lay a hand on him. She chased the dog out the front door, waving the broom furiously.

"Get out of here!" she screamed. "Get out of here! Shoo!"

Hetty King arrived in her buggy with her peace offering—Olivia's flowers—just in time to see pandemonium reign. Janet shot out of the house, screaming and chasing a huge monster of a dog.

"Digger!" Cecily called as she ran from the direction of the barn, covered in grime and dirt. The dog immediately changed course and headed straight for her.

Hetty and Janet watched in horror as the dog ran full tilt into one of the wicker garden tables set with flowers and china, sending everything flying.

"No!" Janet screamed.

Inside the house the baby woke, and his wailing was joined by another cry of panic.

"Sara! Oh no!" It was Olivia's stricken voice.

Hetty looked at Janet and, former arguments forgotten, they ran towards the house.

Chapter Thirteen

Olivia stood and stared at her reflection in the mirror in utter dismay and disbelief. Her wedding dress was the size of a mountain. The creamy, ivory silk hung on her body limply.

Sara looked at her aunt with her mouth open, not knowing what to say, the horror of realization sinking in.

"My wedding is ruined!" Olivia shrieked, and then she started to cry frantically.

"It wasn't my fault, Aunt Olivia," pleaded Sara, almost in tears herself. "Mrs. Lawson read the labels on the box and gave one to me and one to Mrs. Bugle. And Uncle Alec was in a hurry, so I didn't stop to open the box!"

Felicity arrived and was speechless—mostly at the thought of what she would do if this ever happened to her. Janet and Hetty crowded into the room and gaped at the dress in shock.

Olivia saw Hetty's reflection in the mirror and

screamed at her through her tears. "Hetty King! This is all your fault!"

"How could this possibly happen?" Hetty sputtered.

Great-Aunt Eliza arrived in their midst with much tsking and shaking of her head. "No use crying over spilt milk," she said sensibly. "We have work to do."

Hetty grabbed the white box. "It has your name on it!" she cried. "They must have mixed them up in Charlottetown!" She immediately fled from the room, and no one made a move to stop her.

"Oh Janet," Olivia wailed. "Look at it. What am I going to do?"

Janet was at a loss as to how to comfort her, but Eliza held up a needle and thread and set to work.

Alec wearily made his way up the stairs carrying Daniel. He was in the process of thinking to himself that he had seen enough female tears in the last few days to fill the King pond when he was almost knocked down by Hetty as she came tearing past him and out the door. Alec stared and shook his head. Nothing would surprise him ever again.

A buggy appeared around the bend of the winding road that led from the Dale farm. Jasper Dale, resplendent in his wedding suit, held the reins in one hand and a crumpled piece of paper in the other. He was still diligently practicing his speech.

"'My wife, my heaven-sent dove of peace...my ring is the symbol...my ring is the...symbol...'"

He dropped the reins, frantically searching his pockets. He stopped just as suddenly, remembering.

"Felix," he gulped in relief. "That's right... Felix has the ring."

He stuck his finger in his collar, loosening it in the heat, and, clucking to his horse, he continued along the winding road.

From over a hill, another buggy appeared in a cloud of dust, and Jasper watched in amazement as Hetty King shot by him like a bullet, going in the opposite direction.

In a little farmhouse on the outskirts of town, Mrs. Eulalie Bugle and a very ill-looking Cornelia were in the process of opening their precious white box from Charlottetown. They took out the dress and shook it. Cornelia grabbed it from her mother and held it up in front of her, doing an incongruous little waltz step. Only then did her mother discover that it didn't begin to cover half of her.

"Lord love us!" the woman bellowed, so loudly that it wouldn't have surprised anyone if the Lord had heard her, even as far away as Heaven. "It's a size eight, not eighteen!"

Cornelia started to wail. Then she clutched at her stomach and ran from the room.

Hetty's buggy flew through the sagging iron gates of the farm. Pulling mightily on the reins, Hetty brought it to a skidding stop in front of a very surprised Mr. Bugle, who was taking a nap on the front porch.

She raced past the man and into the dingy front hall as he struggled to his feet. Then she charged into the parlor to face an astonished Mrs. Bugle.

"Give me the dress!" Hetty commanded, in a voice she saved for very critical moments in her classroom.

"No!" said Mrs. Bugle, clutching it to her bosom. Cornelia and her father appeared in the doorway, mouths agape.

"It won't fit her!" stated Hetty point-blank, advancing on the woman.

"I'll make it fit," said an equally determined Mrs. Bugle, backing away.

"We have your dress."

"Well, where is it then?"

Hetty made a grab for Olivia's gown and a tug-of-war resulted. Hetty won. Before the Bugles could rally their forces, Hetty was out the door, calling over her shoulder.

"Since Olivia's wedding is first, we will leave

Cornelia's dress at the church to be picked up. Good day."

Hetty departed in a cloud of dust, leaving a speechless and stunned Bugle family standing in a line on their front porch.

"I think I'm gonna be sick, Ma," groaned Cornelia before she raced inside.

Chapter Fourteen

The bells rang joyfully in the steeple of the little white-frame Avonlea Presbyterian Church and echoed through the surrounding hills and valleys. It was 1:30, and guests were beginning to appear on foot and in buggies. They stood in little groups around the church, fanning themselves, the ladies admiring each other's hats and the men talking about the weather and the latest race results from Summerside.

Inside, in the relative coolness of the church, Jasper paced back and forth, consulting his pocket watch. He had, for some reason, been under the impression that the wedding was at one o'clock, not two, and therefore had arrived punctually an hour early. He was already exhausted.

"Nice warm day for you."

Jasper jumped and turned around. It was Reverend Leonard, smiling and holding out his hand. Jasper nodded and shook hands damply, finding suddenly that he wasn't capable of speech.

"Jasper, sit down." Reverend Leonard motioned to the front pew. "Don't wear yourself out."

Jasper nodded again and sat down stiffly.

Just as he did, there was a clattering of feet and Janet King arrived, carrying a crying baby Daniel and corralling Felicity and Cecily into one of the pews. Jasper leapt to his feet to greet her, but Janet took no notice of him at all, so involved was she in family matters.

"Where has Felix got to?" she fretted. "Take Daniel," she said as she handed the baby to a very impatient Felicity.

Felix hung around outside the church door, too hot to go in. He took his handkerchief out of his right pocket and wiped the perspiration from his face. He stuffed it roughly into his left pocket, where his mother had stowed the ring.

Felix was in a terrible mood. He couldn't think of anything worse than being stuck in a church on a Saturday afternoon. Especially a hot Saturday afternoon. He could be swimming or fishing— anything but this. Before he knew what was happening, his daydreams were interrupted by the arrival of the huge, golden dog. It bounded through the gathered guests and made a beeline for Felix, jumping up on him for pure joy, covering his shirt with mud in the process.

"Get down, darn you!" Felix pushed the animal away and then looked down at his shirt. "Oh, great!"

He dragged his handkerchief out of his pocket, not realizing that as he did so, the little band of gold fell to the ground.

Felix attempted to rub the mud off the front of his shirt and succeeded only in smearing it more. His mother, of course, poked her head out of the church door at that very moment, with the expert timing that only comes from years of experience.

"Felix King!" she scolded. "Look at you! Come inside right this minute!"

A wedding was an event in Avonlea, and even the uninvited gathered on the sidelines to see just who was invited, how many were invited, how nervous the groom was, and most important of all, how beautiful the bride's dress was. As the privileged, invited guests filed into the church to find their seats, the moment the remaining crowd outside was waiting for arrived. The buggy containing the bride appeared and pulled up in front of the church amidst hurrahs and cheers.

Olivia was oblivious to her reception. She was sobbing too loudly to hear anyone. Great-Aunt Eliza patted one gloved hand and Sara held on tightly to the other, but no amount of comforting could quell the misery and martyrdom that Olivia was enduring at that moment. This was her big day, the day she had looked forward to ever since Jasper and she had understood that they wanted to spend their lives together. How could it possibly have ended up this way? It was a nightmare come true.

Alec jumped down from the buggy and came round to help the bride out. "You look fine, Olivia. Just fine," he said staunchly, ignoring the fact that even his unpracticed eyes could detect the pins and the tucks that frantic hands had set in place in the hour left before the wedding.

"It's all wrinkled," Olivia wailed as she stood and looked down at the pool of peau-de-soie surrounding her. "Now it'll look even worse!"

"Don't worry, Olivia. You look fine," Alec repeated lamely, holding out his hand to guide her from the buggy.

"I can do it myself," sobbed Olivia, but she leaned on her brother's arm nonetheless.

"You look wonderful," said Alec.

Sara nodded and pasted a bright smile on her face.

Olivia's tears could not be stopped as they hurried her into the church. The crowd of bystanders exchanged glances. They'd seen nervous brides in their day, but this one certainly took the prize. And wasn't her dress a little odd-looking?

Organ music wafted from the little church and the gathering dispersed, thinking that the show was over. But it wasn't. The spectacle of Hetty King, tearing down the road in her buggy like a bat out of hell, her hair flying out behind her, stopped them all in their tracks. She came to a screeching halt in front of them, jumped from the buggy and ran towards the church, wedding gown in hand.

Sara and Great-Aunt Eliza had taken their places next to Janet, and the congregation threw expectant glances towards the back of the church. Jasper stood at the front to one side, next to Reverend Leonard, and the organist was poised to begin the wedding march at Alec's signal. But so far there was no sign of the bride or her brother. Reverend Leonard took a swift look at his watch. If they didn't hurry up, the next wedding party would be upon them.

In the tiny entranceway of the church, behind a closed door and out of sight of the congregation, Olivia was attempting to compose herself. Alec fidgeted nervously, knowing full well that the organist was awaiting his go-ahead sign. Olivia wiped her face with her hankie and took a deep breath. She nodded to Alec to proceed, and he opened the door a notch and signaled to the organist. The music began, and with one last, sobbing intake of breath, Olivia took Alec's arm.

The congregation looked to the back of the church expectantly, but before the bride and her brother could take more than two steps, the church door flew open behind them and Hetty appeared. She grabbed Olivia and Alec and pulled them back, closing the door to the main hall of the church and nodding her head jauntily at the amazed group of wedding guests.

"Hetty! What in blazes are you doing?" whispered Alec.

Without saying a word, Hetty pulled the wrong wedding dress straight up over Olivia's head, leaving her standing in her bloomers in the back of the church. Alec looked away, not quite believing what was happening. Just as quickly, Hetty pulled the right dress over her sister's head and began fastening the hooks and eyes up the back. Olivia was so shocked she could say nothing, but gradually she realized that somehow, somewhere, Hetty had found her proper dress. And it fit! Perfectly!

"Now," Hetty said matter-of-factly, "let me have a look at you." She held Olivia out at arm's length and helped straighten her hair.

A smile shone through Olivia's tears, but there was no time to say anything. The organist began to play the wedding march, and with a tiny push from Hetty, a slightly stunned Olivia started up the aisle on Alec's arm, as beautiful as if she had been preparing for this moment forever.

The guests turned once again, and a communal sigh seemed to fill the little building. What a beautiful bride! Olivia floated between the flower-lined pews, approaching a beaming Jasper. Sara and Great-Aunt Eliza exchanged amazed glances. Somewhere between the buggy and the procession, a true miracle had taken place.

Chapter Fifteen

It was a beautiful wedding. Olivia and Jasper stared lovingly into each other's eyes, and suddenly all the nervous preparations and misgivings were far behind them. The ivory silk of Olivia's dress made her complexion look even more alabaster than ever. The ten-foot train stretched gracefully behind her into the aisle. A wreath of orange blossoms encircled her upswept hair, and a gossamer veil floated around her face and down to meet the train.

Hetty had certainly done herself proud with the floral arrangements. Each pew was adorned with beautiful pink and white roses against a background of evergreen, tied together with white satin and lace bows.

Alec did his duty and gave the bride away without a slip-up. He then took his seat next to Janet, but found that his wife was still annoyed with him and refused to return the squeeze he gave her hand. Felix stood behind the happy couple waiting his turn to play his vital role.

The congregation watched in silent admiration. The only sound came from the King pew as baby Daniel fussed and cried and was passed from hand to hand until he reached Great-Aunt Eliza and settled completely.

"I, Olivia King, take thee, Jasper Dale, to be my lawful wedded husband, according to God's Holy Ordinance. To have and to hold from this day forward, for better, for worse…"

Her Aunt Olivia had never looked so beautiful as she did at this moment, thought Sara. A tear rolled down Hetty's cheek as she listened to Olivia exchange vows with Jasper.

Bolstered by sudden confidence that all would be well, Jasper repeated his vows after Reverend

Leonard without a flaw, in a firm and steady voice that carried to the back of the flower-filled church.

"...for richer, for poorer, in sickness and in health, to forsake all others and to love and to cherish, till death do us part."

"Could we have the ring, please?"

Felix jumped. He had been in the middle of a daydream, and Reverend Leonard had to repeat his request. Jasper turned around expectantly as Felix felt in his pocket. There was nothing there. He tried the other pocket, with no luck. Felix began to panic. He looked frantically over his shoulder at his mother.

"Felix, it's in your left pocket! Your left!" hissed Janet.

Felix felt deep into the left and the right once again, turning his pockets inside out. "It isn't! I checked!"

The congregation buzzed, and Janet and Hetty converged on a very upset Felix.

"I didn't lose it!" he protested. "Honest!" He started to cry with embarrassment. "I didn't touch it!"

Janet and Hetty tried to calm him down, at the same time assuring themselves that the ring was, in fact, gone.

Janet looked down at her own gold band and caught Hetty's pleading glance. She struggled with her ring for what seemed like forever, and it finally came off. She handed it to Felix. Felix handed it to Jasper. Jasper gave it to Reverend Leonard. Reverend Leonard handed it back to Jasper and nodded for him to go on. Jasper stared at him blankly.

"I give this ring..." the poor Reverend prompted in a low voice.

Jasper leapt back to the matter at hand. "I give this ring..." he began as he slid Janet's gold band on Olivia's finger, "as a token and pledge...of the covenant now made between us."

Olivia looked at the ring, and then up into Jasper's eyes, and smiled.

"For as much as Olivia and Jasper have consented together in holy wedlock and have declared the same before God and in the presence of these witnesses; I pronounce you man and wife, in the name of the Father, the Son and the Holy Ghost. Amen. Jasper, you may kiss your bride."

Jasper didn't know how he ever did it, but he did kiss his bride—right in front of everyone, something he would have believed impossible not many months before.

The organist hit the keys with the enthusiasm of a racehorse having finally heard the starting bell. The recessional music rang out through the church and Jasper and Olivia made their way down the aisle, smiling and holding on to each other for dear life. Sara glanced at her Aunt Hetty and was not surprised to see tears rolling down her cheeks.

The happy couple emerged from the church and into the sunshine and was immediately followed by friends and relations wishing them well and throwing handfuls of rice.

In the middle of the gaiety, another buggy pulled up, and Mrs. Bugle and Cornelia tumbled out of it. They pushed through the crowds with impatience, determined to confront Hetty King and demand the dress. Cornelia, however, saw something shining in the grass. She stooped down to pick it up.

Hetty walked down the aisle of the now empty and silent church and methodically stripped the pews of all their flowers. She certainly wasn't going to do any favors for that Bugle woman, not after all the trouble she had caused. A shadow fell over the room, and Mrs. Bugle herself appeared in the doorway, her hands on her hips. Hetty appraised her coolly and very calmly handed over the dress. Before the woman could say anything, her daughter joined her.

"Look, Ma, it's a ring." She held the small band of gold in the sunlight that poured through the church door.

Hetty did no more than raise an eyebrow.

"Thank you, so much," she merely said, and she plucked it from the girl's chubby hand. She continued on her way, leaving the pair staring.

Chapter Sixteen

The entire King clan lined up under the apple trees to have their photograph taken. A spot next to a smiling Olivia was noticeably empty until Jasper suddenly popped out from under the black velvet cloth of the camera and ran like the devil to take his place. He arrived beside Olivia just as the flash exploded. Everyone applauded his feat, and the group broke up to get down to the most important part of the reception—the food.

Janet and Alec had stood beside one another, smiling broadly, until the flash went off. Then the smiles were replaced by icy coolness. Felicity and Felix exchanged looks. Their parents were acting very oddly indeed.

The garden looked picture perfect. The guests sat at the white wicker tables and chairs, enjoying the delicious fare that Janet had slaved for days to prepare. Beautiful china platters overflowed with tiny sandwiches filled with turkey, ham, cream cheese, cucumber and lettuce. Deviled eggs were devoured, along with salads, homemade bread and rolls, fresh apple turnovers and, of course, the wedding cake. It was admired by all, and Janet had to admit, no one could see where she had patched the icing after the horrible incident with that dog. She shuddered to think about it.

Olivia and Jasper sat at the dreaded head table and found to their amazement that they were enjoying themselves immensely. It was a good view, as Jasper had jokingly suggested. They could look out over all their guests and see them laughing and talking and obviously enjoying themselves. At the moment, their audience was chuckling and good-naturedly ribbing Alec, who had risen to make his speech to Olivia and Jasper.

"And so," he concluded, "as you start your journey into married life, and believe me, it's an adventurous one ..." he paused and looked at Janet, who smiled politely and bowed her head. Alec continued, "We would like to wish you both the very best."

Alec raised his glass of cordial and the guests all toasted the bride and groom. He sat down amid cheers and spoons clattering against glasses. From her table in front of Olivia and Jasper, Sara tried to get the groom's attention.

"Jasper!" she whispered to him. He turned from his conversation with Hetty, who sat on his left, and looked down at Sara's insistent face. "Now!" she hissed. "Now's your chance!"

Jasper frowned and shook his head slightly. He knew what she meant, but he wasn't sure that he was ready. He wasn't sure he would ever be ready.

"Please! Do it!" Sara pointed to a sheet of paper in her hand. "Go! Now!"

Jasper took a deep breath. Sara was right, of course. There was no time like the present. If he didn't follow through today on his promise to himself, he knew he would never forgive himself tomorrow.

Jasper stood up, and gradually the guests realized he was standing for a reason, not just to stretch his legs. The crowd slowly quieted down until there was a slightly uncomfortable silence.

Jasper cleared his throat nervously. "I...I...I'd just like to take this opportunity...to say a few words to my new...wi...wi..." The word wouldn't come. "To Olivia."

Sara nodded encouragingly at him. Felicity and Felix began to giggle, and she looked daggers at them.

Jasper looked down and painfully searched through his memory for the speech he had prepared.

"To my bride," he began tentatively. "How can I describe the many ways I love thee?"

At his side, Hetty pressed her temples with her fingertips. The only word that came to her mind was "why?"

"My...my..." Jasper's mind went blank, and a slow red started to creep from the top of his stiffly starched collar.

Sara sensed his confusion and mouthed the word "love" several times until he finally got it.

"My love, my…" He stopped again, and the guests shifted uncomfortably. Olivia looked down at her hands, suffering along with her new husband. Sara mouthed the word "life."

"My…life, my…" Jasper continued haltingly. He finally stopped. He looked at Sara apologetically. "No," he said quietly, as much to himself as to anyone else. "I'm going to say it my own way, in my own…words."

Once again, Jasper cleared his throat. He glanced down at Olivia and then looked out at the waiting faces of his audience.

"Falling in love with Olivia…" he began quietly, "and even more unbelievable, her falling in love with me…was the most amazing and wonderful thing that could possibly have ever happened to me. It's the truth, Olivia." He turned and looked directly at his radiant new bride. "You are the most…you are the most…special person…"

Almost overcome, he looked back to his enraptured audience. "Now, I know how the Kings rally together to look after their own…there isn't a stronger or more loyal family on the Island… and," he paused for a moment, "I want to assure you all that I am not taking Olivia away from this fine, solid family of hers, but rather, that I am honored to become a part of it."

Hetty bit her lip, surprised at the sudden choking feeling in her throat. She felt Alec, on her other side, take her hand and squeeze it hard. She squeezed back and smiled up at Jasper.

"I'd like to propose a toast to my beautiful, new bride…who means more to me than…well…anything in the whole world. To Olivia."

Not once had Jasper Dale stumbled or stuttered. Everyone raised their glasses.

"To Olivia."

Tears streamed down Olivia's cheeks. Sara smiled at Jasper and gave him the thumbs-up. Then she happened to glance at her Aunt Hetty, whose face betrayed how moved she was by Jasper's words. Janet and Alec had also exchanged many looks throughout Jasper's speech, and at its end, they reached out and held hands. It had not gone unnoticed by Felix, who dug Felicity in the ribs. They watched as their father took something out of his pocket. He leaned over to Janet and whispered in her ear.

"For better or for worse?"

He slipped her gold band back on her finger where it belonged. It was Janet's turn to get teary-eyed.

Felix beamed as he watched his parents embrace. Cecily smiled and, reaching down under the table, patted the golden head of the dog that lay at her feet, hidden by the long tablecloth. Now that her parents had made up, she felt sure Digger's future was secure.

Felicity smiled, too, but not for long, as Daniel, sitting on her lap, chose that precise moment to start screaming. Eliza had been holding court at another table, but she excused herself grandly and came to Felicity's rescue. She hadn't missed Alec and Janet's kiss either and thought it scandalous. "You'd think *they* were the newlyweds!" she couldn't help commenting to anyone who would listen.

The guests burst into applause for Olivia and Jasper, and, amid the banging of forks and spoons on one hundred and twenty-two glasses, not counting the bride and groom, the happy couple finally succumbed and, standing up, kissed each other for the whole world to see.

Chapter Seventeen

The last of the guests had packed themselves into their buggies, vowing that they had never seen a more beautiful wedding or been to a better reception and they couldn't imagine eating another bite for weeks. The sun was close to the horizon as they meandered homeward, leaving a massive clean-up job for every able-bodied member of the King family.

Hetty King had taken refuge in the kitchen and stood by the sink, rinsing dishes, a faraway look in her eye.

"There you are!" It was Olivia, dressed in her traveling clothes, a charming hand-embroidered white organza blouse tucked into a beautifully cut, high-waisted ivory wool skirt that accentuated her narrow waistline. White gloves with tiny pearl buttons and a matching ivory hat trimmed with soft-pink silk roses completed her outfit.

Hetty turned to her sister with a small, sheepish smile. "Oh. Hello, Olivia." She motioned to the sink full of dishes. "Just trying to make myself useful." She turned quickly back to the job at hand, her shoulders and back stiff with emotion.

"Hetty..." Olivia paused and bit her lip, not sure what to say or how to say it. "I just...I just want you to know that the wedding was a wonderful idea. It wouldn't have been right to be married without my family surrounding me."

There was a short silence. "For all the trouble we've been through, I should have let you elope in the first place," Hetty said quietly.

She turned to see Olivia smiling. Their mutual chuckle broke the ice and they threw themselves into each other's arms.

"I'm going to miss you and Rose Cottage so much," gasped Olivia as the full reality of the situation hit her.

Hetty swallowed hard, trying desperately to get rid of the lump in her throat. "Rose Cottage is not going anywhere. It will always be there for you. So will I," she said brusquely, attempting to hide her wavering emotions. She was remembering her conversation with Alec, and she realized that he had been right. She wasn't losing Olivia. The ties that bound them were far stronger than that.

Looking out the window, she spotted Jasper waiting with Sara by his buggy.

"Well, you'd better be on your way. Your new husband is waiting."

Olivia grinned at her sister through her tears and nodded.

"And Olivia," Hetty added. "For all his obvious shortcomings, Jasper has come a long way since he met you. You've made a sow's ear into a silk purse."

Jasper watched as Olivia walked towards him across the lawn, smiling, her arm linked with Hetty's. Janet held out her arms to Olivia, who hugged her and thanked her for all she had done. Then she said her goodbyes to Alec and the children. Her eyes filled with tears once again as she gave one last, long hug to Hetty and Sara, but the minute Jasper appeared by her side to help her into the buggy, she was all smiles, ready to start a new chapter of her life—as a married woman.

Just as Jasper was about to take his seat beside his bride, Alec gave Hetty a bit of a push, and she found herself face to face with her new brother-in-law.

"Congratulations, Jasper," she said, holding out her hand. "Welcome to the family." Impulsively, to the great surprise of both of them, she gave him a quick hug and an impetuous peck on the cheek.

"Thank you...Hetty," the poor fellow stammered, and, quite taken aback, he flung himself up into the driver's seat.

Olivia blew a kiss, calling her goodbyes, but family business was not yet concluded. Great-Aunt Eliza, who had been very quiet throughout the entire ceremony and reception, chose that moment to impart to Olivia the wisdom she had gained throughout her many years as a spinster. She pulled the bride down to her and whispered in her ear.

"A man is nothing but trouble, Olivia, and, of all the uncertain things in this world, marriage is the most uncertain. Remember that."

Olivia tried very hard not to burst out into wild laughter. Instead, she pinned her most serious look on her face.

"I will, Aunt Eliza," she promised. "Thank you for the advice."

Both Jasper and Olivia smiled and waved to everyone as the buggy moved forward down the driveway of the King farm. The "Just Married" sign jiggled and bumped as they turned onto the road and the chorus of goodbyes echoed in the warm June air. As the buggy finally disappeared behind a hill, Hetty and Sara stood together, alone, holding hands and waving.

🍒　🍒　🍒